...  o make out t... *pitch sound had that deep pitch, but not the sound. Listening to him left her feeling alive, tingling from head to toe. Its timbre coursed through her the same as it had since the first night she'd invited herself to his table and sat down.*

From his private corner, he'd watched her each night, sipping on his illegal whiskey, piercing her with eyes that matched his drink. Never having more than one, and always alone except for times she would meander over and tease a smile from those firm lips.

When the music hit her veins, the words that flowed from her mouth were directed to him. No wonder his regular seat was empty. Harry Dempsey must have been the man with whom Butch was speaking.

"Dempsey." Joey's tone held an edge of fear. "The...uh...dame took a wrong turn."

Harry moved in her direction, his gait slow, deliberate, until he stood within touching distance. "Dame?" That single word rang through the abandoned space.

Oh no. Meggie launched herself from her hiding place and threw her arms about Harry's neck. Locked in his muscular embrace, she rested her chin on his shoulder. His arms tightened around her. "Oh, Harry. I came as fast as I could. Just as we'd planned." The words, she'd intended to carry, came out breathless. "Fast, huh?" The whisper was against her ear where no one else could hear, raised goose prickles over her entire body. "Guess I'll have to do something about that." He lifted his head.

copyright © 2015 by Kathy L Wheeler

All Rights Reserved

http://kathylwheeler.com

These stories are works of fiction. Names, characters, places and incidents are either products of the author's imagination used fictitiously. Any resemblance to actual events, locales, or persons, living or dead, is entirely coincidental.

All rights reserved.
No part of this publication can be reproduced or transmitted in any form or by any means, electronic or mechanical, without permission in writing from Kathy L Wheeler.

Cover Art © Kelli McBride

Reckless

Kathy L Wheeler

Acknowledgements

Our Martini Club has been a "thing" going on for some four years now. I suppose the idea to start a series of stories was a bit of joke that eventually turned into something tangible. Through our many critique sessions, Martini Club meetings, and various retreats Amanda McCabe, Alicia Dean, Krysta Scott and I found a way to complete this first series of truly fun stories. And while it has taken longer than we'd planned from inspiration to publication, I can honestly say, I am honored to be a part of such a creative and loving group of women I will count as great friends for the rest of my life. Thank you, girls for being the best critique partners, authors and best friends a person could dream of having.

I don't want to forget our honorary member Cindy Sorenson, who is a fabulous writing talent of YA in her own right and J. Lynn McKay who took time out of her busy schedule to read and edit and give excellent feedback. Nor do I want to forget the Martini Lounge in Edmond who cater to our every need and want. We LOVE you, and hope to continue our impromptus for many years to come.

Prologue

EYES CLOSED, LADY MARGARET Montley glided her fingers across ivory keys of the ancient grand piano. Her voice slid into a pivotal cadence that marked the unusual piece of a 12 bar blues tune. Poignant notes that echoed against the hardwood floors and walls in the Duke of Winsome family's large ballroom. The single cheer in the form of applause startled Meggie.

Her eyes snapped open, meeting the matched pair blues of the dowager's. A force of nature, her mother. Slim, petite and accustomed to everything in her perfect world go according to her perfect plan. And then there was her only daughter, Meggie...

"That was lovely, dear. But couldn't you sing something a bit more..." Her hand flitted out. "...a bit less..." Her mother smiled in her sweet, yet condescending way. "Something lively and upbeat, not like that new—"

"Jazz, mother. It's jazz, and it suits me *perfectly*."

"I'm not complaining, darling. You have a lovely voice. You play flawlessly. I just don't see you impressing a man—" she cleared her throat. "—a *decent* man, singing such suggestive tunes."

Meggie bit back her irritation. It was an age old argument. *There is no need to continue practicing, dear. Things are different now than in my day when one needed one's talents to impress a gentleman. With your beauty, all you need do is smile and they shall stampede the entry hall.*

Her older brother by a mere four minutes strolled into the ballroom, empty but for the piano. "Hey, Pegs."

The name sent Meggie's blood pressure to percolating. He knew just how to crawl under her skin. "Do. Not. Call. Me. That."

"Hi, Mums."

"Garrett, darling, when did you arrive?"

"Just this minute. Where are the others?" Garrett was stocky with hair the same blond as her own, and the same blue eyes as all of the Montleys. He was also the one sibling who knew her best. And with her and Jessie's plans to escape choke-holding England—after Jessie's sister's wedding, Meggie had to take extreme caution or their adventure would be lost before it had begun.

Garrett sauntered across the ballroom and kissed her cheek. "I heard you from the foyer, Megs. You sound good. Real fine."

Just like that her heart melted. She would miss him terribly. "Thank you, Garrett."

"Don't encourage her, darling. She has notions of singing—*in public.*" A delicate shudder wracked her mother's body.

Garrett shot Meggie a wink. "Don't worry, Mums. We'll get your girl here shackled before you know it."

Meggie's hands clenched. How easily her family dismissed her dreams, her ambitions. As if she were some empty headed piece to be moved about a chessboard.

Meggie's two older siblings, Samuel and Ross, meandered in. Samuel and Ross, were dark where Garrett and Meggie were fair. But all three of her brothers were over the top attractive, never lacking for feminine company.

Her mother's smile brightened. A genuine smile that stole Meggie's breath, leaving her mother looking as if she floated on clouds.

"Meggie, Mums is right. You shouldn't be singing that jazzy, blues stuff. It's much too serious and provocative."

Meggie's lips tightened as her mother gasped and tapped him on the arm. "Watch your language in mixed company, Samuel."

"You forgot *your grace*." Meggie muttered under her breath, as her sarcasm was never well received. Since Sam had stepped into their father's title some three years past, it seemed her once carefree brother's nature had been buried right along with Papa.

His lips curled. It was a weak smile at best. "Is it time for supper?"

"Yes, we're famished. I've a boxing match to attend, followed by a late night at the theater." Ross never seemed to have an opinion on Meggie's pastime. And at the moment she was profoundly grateful.

"Fifteen minutes. You know the routine. Sherry in the west parlor first. Wash up." Mother shooed them out.

So, why did Mother insist Meggie be the one to marry? This was the twentieth century. Shouldn't *she* be allowed the freedom to act on her hopes and dreams? Samuel, despite being heir to the duke, had studied law. And Garrett had been accepted to a prestigious art school in Paris. He was set to leave just after the wedding. She wrinkled her nose. Ross, however, had no dreams that she could discern. Neither he nor that lazy scoundrel, Percy, he always hung about.

The *gentleman* Mother expected Meggie to marry.

She shuddered. Just the thought of those thin lips coming near her was enough to send her swimming across the Atlantic before Lulu's wedding. She wondered if Percy was privy to her mother's designs. Doubtful, as he and Ross spent most of their time at the race track and gambling halls.

All Meggie dreamed her whole life was to sing—and perhaps act, but she was most careful in hiding that particular ambition. Mother would likely perish at the idea.

"Come along, Margaret. Your brothers have plans tonight."

"Yes, Mother," she murmured. Her time would be here soon enough. After all, the wedding was but two days away.

Three days later

MEGGIE COULDN'T BELIEVE IT. She, Jessie and Lady Charlotte Leighton, or Charli as she preferred now that she was embarking on a new life too, were just blocks from walking up the gangplank to freedom. A new start. No more innuendoes from her mother and brothers. If they could just make it to the ship without Charli giving them away.

"Don't look so terrified, Charli." Meggie tried to curb her irritation. Charli couldn't help being so shy. "This is an adventure."

Jessie looped her arm through Charli's. "You'll see. We'll have a grand time. You won't have to marry that stodgy Lord Brigdon. In no time at all you'll be baking, not just the best scones Americans have ever tasted, but the best cakes, and pastries for the most lavish parties imaginable."

Meggie had to give Charli credit as she tried smiling through her fear, yet not quite managing the feat.

"I'd just feel better if we'd brought a maid or...or *some* companion." Her voice trembled.

Meggie was careful to keep her tone gentle. "You know we couldn't have dared trusting anyone." They hadn't boarded the *Empress of India* yet. Not all danger lay around the London docks. Samuel's dukedom could stifle their plans as effectively as murder.

Thick fog hovered low in the early grey morning skies. A shudder skittered up Meggie's spine. "Let's hurry," she said, broadening her steps.

Activity picked up the closer they grew to the water, along with the stench. All conversation stalled, and Meggie gripped the handle of her bag as they made their way briskly down the street.

"No!" The voice reached through the dense atmosphere a mere block from their destination.

"Come on, love. I'll be gentle," the words slurred heavily.

Meggie stopped.

"What are you doing?" Charli whispered, her voice as alarmed as the girl Meggie was trying to discern through the soupy sky.

"We have to help," she whispered back.

"Oh, Megs." Jessie rolled her eyes—Meggie could hear it in her voice.

At least Jessie would understand. If Meggie hadn't stopped she had no doubt Jess would have.

"Let me go. Let. Me. Go." The panicked pitch rose two octaves.

"She's over there," Meggie said. "In that doorway." Meggie lifted her skirt and ran, briefly picturing her mother's horror. Jess and Charli's footsteps pounded behind. She followed the frightened sound, pausing before an abandoned shop.

A tall, lanky man hunched over a girl who tried to crouch away, his hand gripping her breast.

Meggie dropped her valise. The sound carried in the quiet street. "There you are, you silly girl. You scared us, getting separated like that."

Luckily, the girl lost no time in picking up the ruse. She shoved away the brute's hand and brought up her knee. His pained high-pitched cry erupted. To Meggie's surprise, he stumbled, tripping back and falling into a fetal position. A remarkable move, really. Something to ask the cheeky girl about later. Meggie grabbed her hand, snatched up her bag and took off, the other girls quickly following.

A half block from the ship, Meggie bent to catch her breath, taking in the girl's matted hair and dirt-streaked face.

"Thank you, milady." Her lips trembled though she put up a brave front.

"The name is Meggie. This is Jess—" She indicated with one hand. "And Charli. What's yours?"

"Eliza."

"Well, Eliza. The docks aren't safe for a girl alone. Where are you going?"

"The same as you I imagine."

"You're going to America?" Excitement spilled from Jessie. "That's brilliant."

The girl's gaze flitted away. "Um, uh, y-yes."

Charli frowned. "Alone?"

Meggie narrowed her eyes on her wrinkled frock where something suspicious streaked across the bodice. She prayed it was mud. This girl was in trouble, something Meggie and Jess were no strangers to. "You'll come with us."

"Oh, I couldn't possibly—"

"Of course you can. We need a fourth, besides." That settled, Meggie took her arm once more, leaving Jess to handle Charli. "We're on an adventure."

One

New York City — Six months later

"YOU DON'T KNOW WHAT you are saying, *Lady* Margaret."

That hurt. Meggie thought they were better friends than the mere acquaintances Eliza had just insinuated with her formal address. She hadn't been acknowledged as Lady Margaret—in the actual title form—since the day she, Lady Jessica Hatton, Lady Charlotte Leighton and Eliza Gilbert rushed up the gangplank of the *Empress of India* in their haste to depart England over six months ago.

"Eliza, it's after three in the morning, and you have a split lip." Just the sight of Eliza's blood drew the image of Roxy, the girl found murdered in the alley behind Club 501. "I only want to help."

Eliza's greenish-brown eyes flashed. The small, dark beauty mark on her right cheek, standing out, stark, on her pale skin. She marched across the small living area, back and forth, her slender frame seeming unable to convey her anger or worry. Meggie had trouble discerning which.

The tiny flat they shared with Jess and Charli was just that—tiny. Eliza's cropped, chestnut hair in soft finger waves swung with each turn. After her third or fourth turn about the room, she stopped and faced Meggie, hands fisted at her hips. Frustration covered her pert features. And fear, Meggie decided. Deep-reaching fear lay beneath her tough exterior.

Eliza's teeth tugged at her bottom lip—another sign of her angst. "You don't understand, Meggie. I can't let you help. This is *my* predicament and the cost is too much." Her gaze flew to the window over the small worn sofa, fingers rubbing a pendant she wore around her neck.

Meggie rose from the sofa and grasped her friend's hands. Ice cold. "What is it? I'm certain we can help."

Panic seared her features. "No! You mustn't say anything. To anyone. Promise me, Meggie."

"Of course, I promise. Nothing can be so dire to warrant this sort of distress." She would promise anything to assure Eliza. But Meggie refused to leave her friend in peril without doing *something*. "You must tell me what happened."

Eliza pulled her hands away and went to the grimy window and looked out. "I-I fell," she said.

Meggie could spot a lie a mile away. All hers and Jess's nonsense when they were at Mrs. Greensley's School for Young Ladies had taught her well. Like the time they'd stuffed glue in the locks on finals day, then batting their eyes, proclaiming their innocence to Monsieur Duclaric, who'd certainly suspected. Though, eventually, they were found out and reprimanded but good. She still wasn't sure how the French Instructor had discovered the truth, to this day.

La! The bunk she and Jess handed Lady Hatton on a regular basis? Why, their half-truths and white lies kept them out of more scrapes than Meggie could count. Yes, for a *Lady* Meggie knew a thing or two about getting in and out of trouble. Eliza was not telling all.

Meggie steeled her resolve, despite her heart wanting to relent, and let her impatience through. "Blast, it, Eliza. If you don't tell me the truth right this minute then I shall call the constable."

"You wouldn't," she whispered.

"I would. Now, spill."

Eliza turned from the window, eyes glittering with tears. "The-the job with Oscar isn't quite as…as grand as I first believed."

Meggie was afraid of that. "Is he the one who hurt you?"

Eliza lips tightened, but she didn't speak.

Meggie's heart went out to her. "Oh, darling, he is, isn't he? Please, tell me what's going on. I can't help if I don't know." She tugged her friend to the tattered sofa.

Eliza swooped her pocketbook from the cushion and gripped it, knuckles white. She worked the clasp open and closed, over and over, sniffing back tears. "It's fine, truly. I just thought it would be…"

A chill stole up Meggie's spine. "What, Eliza? You never answered my question. *Did* he hurt you?"

"No, it's just as I said." The words came quickly. "I f-fell. I just believed the work—the work would be a little more…glamorous." She glanced out the window again, inhaled deeply, then turned back. Squared her shoulders. "Truly, Meggie. I'm fine. It really is a grand o-opportunity." Her stutter was another sure sign there was more to that story.

"But?"

Eliza gazed out the window again but Meggie felt certain she saw nothing beyond the sheer curtain. It was dark, and no moon filtered through the thick clouds. Her gaze grew unfocused, as if her mind had drifted elsewhere—somewhere unpleasant. "I didn't realize I would be expected to…" She took another deep breath. "…to…to date…some of the guests." The words ended on a whisper and her gaze fell to the purse in her lap. She seemed surprised to see it there.

"Date," Meggie repeated slowly. "Eliza, you're not—what I mean is, you aren't—" The ghastly thought stuck in her throat, but she forged on. "—you haven't been—" She inhaled deeply. "Are you—*prostituting* yourself?" The last came out in a horrified whisper.

Eliza's hazel eyes darkened with anger. She shot to her feet, knocking her pocketbook to the floor. "Of course not! How dare you suggest such a thing."

Meggie dropped to the floor to help gather—she picked up a fat wad of bills, looked up at Eliza, whose already pale face turned bloodless. Meggie stood slowly and held the money in her outstretched palm. Eliza snatched away the wad and squatted to swoop up the rest of the contents that had spilled.

"It—it's my pay for last week," Eliza mumbled, standing.

Shock then certainty ricocheted through Meggie. She'd never seen so much cash. "Oh, Eliza." She took her friend's cold hands in hers, forced her to meet her eyes. "I know there is more going on than you are sharing." Meggie pulled herself up, infused her voice with her usual confidence. "You must leave his employ immediately. We'll help you. All of us. Charli, Jess, and I, until you find some other position."

The tears shimmering in her eyes broke Meggie's heart. "You've done so much for me already. I'm the daughter of a *housekeeper,* Meggie. The three of you—you're ladies. You've taken me in, helped pay my way." She shook her head and the tears slid down her cheeks. "How can I bear not doing my part?" She dashed them away, drew in an audible breath and dropped her eyes. "Besides, I-I can't just…leave any time I choose."

"Don't be ridiculous. Of course you can. He doesn't *own* you." Meggie was furious. How dare Mr. Cummings treat one of Meggie's friends like a common...common harlot!

Eliza shrugged away, shoulders hunched, looked out at the dark night again. "Actually, he does. I…I signed a contract. I'm obligated to remain for two years. Unless I can pay the termination fee." She turned back to Meggie, her bottom lip trembling.

The sight incited Meggie further. "That's bunk, Eliza. The man is treating you like a slave." This is what came for people who were taught no better than to believe they should be indentured for life. Meggie pulled back her shoulders and lifted her chin. "It's probably less trouble to just pay his damned extortion fees. All of us will chip in, and with the funds you have there..." Meg nodded toward her pocketbook, "How much is the scoundrel demanding?"

Eliza grimaced, tiny lines appearing around her lips. "A thousand dollars."

Meggie fell back onto the sofa, feeling faint. "A-a thousand?"

CLUB 501 WAS HOPPING. THE tucked-away speakeasy on the lower end of Broadway in Manhattan with its soft ambience in muted gold lighting splayed against dark grained wood was most elegant. Flappers and socialites decorated the arms of dapper young men. A crowd of aristocrats, upper echelons and a theater throng, all of which had hit the doors less than an hour ago. A small grin touched her. If only her mother and brothers could see her now. Not everyone in this speakeasy was here just for the hooch. They'd come to see her too. Take that lovely Harry Dempsey for example. He sat at his regular corner table barely drinking at all. Eyes the color of whiskey with depths of promised secrets that had her crooning her deepest desires in his direction.

Meggie let out a stream of air, her feet already aching at their first break of the night. "I'll be back in a jiff, Freddie," she said to the young trumpet player. She hurried to the bar and called out, "Ginger ale, Ira."

Worry gripped her. She had to somehow find a way to help Eliza. Though Jess, Charli and Meggie had found Eliza near on the London docks, there was a certain innocence about her that drew men in her direction. Men like that awful Oscar Cummings. Meggie pushed her way through the crowd to the ladies room. Not an easy task, navigating such a mob.

She reached for the handle but was snagged by the waist.

"Where's you headed, doll face?" Gin-saturated stench that could likely take out half the crowd as quick as a round from Machine Gun Kelly's chopper hit her nostrils.

Something about Joey Keagan raised the fine hairs at her nape. The weasel's short black hair was parted on one side and slicked down. Sure, some might find him attractive enough, but Meggie thought him a bit off. Like tonight, wearing knickers that fell just below his knees, but the perfect match between his red and green argyle socks and sweater were a bit of a stretch.

Well, Christmas was but a month or so away...

She shoved against his chest and stepped back. "Retiring room, Joey." Confusion covered his drunk-filled gaze, before understanding set in. She rolled her eyes.

"Ah, the john." He leaned in and licked the lobe of her ear. She gasped but he spoke over it. "I'll bet the swells never tire of that purty English lilt you sprout. Go on then. I'll be here waitin' for you when you come back."

"Perfect," she muttered under her breath, making her escape. Despite the speakeasy clientele being upscale, there were still the creepers. Meggie cringed at her snobbish thoughts. Unlike her mother's beliefs, class was something a person should be able to earn. Not be handed to them due to their circumstances of birth. Just look at Percy.

She took care of business quickly, scrubbing away the touch of Joey's disgusting thin lips and shuddered. It would be a cold day in hell before that bastard touched her again. She'd flatten the sap, just see if she didn't.

Her reflection in the mirror showed her blonde curls a little worse for wear, so she fluffed them up. The new sleeked down styles didn't flatter her heart-shaped face in the least. Not that it mattered. She wore her hair to her shoulders—a style that would send her mother into an apoplectic fit—in curls that acted of their own accord. She reapplied her red lip-stain, carefully maintaining the Cupid's bow effect. After adjusting her dress, straightening her stockings, pinching her cheeks—until surely, she'd dawdled long enough to out wait Joey-the creep-Keagan, she went to the door and peered out, looking both left then right.

Relief rushed out in a quick breath. Joey was nowhere in sight. The club crowd was thicker. The shows in Times Square must have let out and patrons kept piling in. She edged her way to the bar for her Ginger-ale. Before she made it, some corked sot plowed into her, upsetting her balance in her uncomfortable t-strap pumps. The drunk's hands closed around her upper arms from behind. Joey's nasally pitch sounded in her ear. "What's eatin' you, doll face?"

Hysteria clogged her throat with an onslaught of nausea as Joey's gin-reeked breath reached her nostrils. Another shudder skittered up her spine. She'd thought him nice enough as blokes went but that sentimentality flew away along with her calm demeanor as she struggled against his tightening grip.

Her glance snapped to the corner, to Harry Dempsey's regular spot. Empty.

He was always there when the set started. Not only did his tranquility center her before each performance, and she suspected he had a hand in keeping the Joey Keagans' at bay, she was utterly and completely enthralled with him. But where was he when she needed him?

She squelched her panic, swallowed her screams. "You shouldn't call me that." Joey was always tossing out the odd innuendo she rarely understood.

He spun her around, his smug grin shifting her panic into fury.

"What makes you think something is "eating me"?" The leer he turned on her set her cheeks aflame. "Let go of me."

"Come on, doll. You don't mean it." Joey's dark brown eyes softened with desire. He leaned in, breathed on her neck. "We'll make a great team. With your body and my smarts, we can't lose."

He couldn't possibly mean—embarrassment flooded her. Was this what happened to Eliza? Meggie brought her hands up and shoved, but his hold firmed and he nipped her neck. If he were a poisonous viper she'd be dead. "I'll pass, thank you."

He licked the place he bit, making her skin crawl. "Come on, doll. Just think of it. We could make hundreds, thousands—"

Alarm skittered up her spine. She slammed the pointed heel of her shoe onto his foot. His arms dropped so suddenly she flailed back. A push, then drunken slur "hey, watch it" sounded behind. The sot managed to right her, and she grabbed the opportunity, slipping through a paneled door and ran. She flew past stacked boxes of crates, past darkened rooms through a winding hallway that made her dizzy then breathless. She paused at a staircase leading up and listened for him.

Heavy footsteps echoed on the clap boards, and she darted up the stairs of Club 501's inner sanctum to another hallway with very little light guiding her path. The corridor seemed eerily quiet compared to the mob in the club. Meggie clung to the wall, cognizant of the danger she'd just put herself in. Thoughts of that dead girl, Roxy raced through her head with startling clarity. Just over a week ago. Had she been dragged through these very halls first? Fear spiked her pulse along with the sound of the increasing footsteps. She spotted a light ahead and increased her pace.

Meggie paused outside a darkened doorway and slipped off her heels, then tip-toed by. All she could see was the back of Butch Weaver's shiny bald head, hunched over, counting a stack of bills that took her breath away.

Money that could help Eliza. Where had it all come from? Butch murmured something to someone she couldn't see. Joey's footsteps pounded the wood planks. Meggie slipped past the office to the next door and twisted the knob. Locked.

She hurried on. A second later she stumbled into the large open area of an abandoned warehouse. She glanced around and spotted several stacked casks, lining the end of the hallway near open doors, where a large truck was backed in.

Meggie ran over and squeezed between the first two casks she could fit between, certain her red dress rivaled a beacon. She would leave screaming for help as the last option. Nothing irritated her more than having to shriek for help. Having three brothers did that to a girl.

She plastered against the large barrels just as Joey filed into view. She held her breath.

"Come on, doll," Joey called softly.

The bastard. How she wished it had been his face she'd stomped instead of his foot. She'd rub his nose in his own blood. Gads, her brother always accused her of being somewhat more bloodthirsty than the norm.

Meggie's heart pounded so hard it vibrated through her spine to the wood barrels at her back. The breeze whipped through the casks, stirring her skirt. She tried to snatch it back but it billowed out like a cape before an enraged bull.

Joey's maniacal chuckle chilled her inside out, his steps gliding toward her. Now she was well and truly trapped.

"Keagan. What the fuck are you doing back here?" The dark growling voice demanded.

Meggie leaned forward. The light was too dim to make out the expression behind that deep pitch, but not the sound. Listening to him left her feeling alive, tingling from head to toe. Its timbre coursed through her the same as it had since the first night she'd invited herself to his table and sat down.

From his private corner, he'd watched her each night, sipping on his illegal whiskey, piercing her with eyes that matched his drink. Never having more than one, and always alone except for times she would meander over and tease a smile from those firm lips.

When the music hit her veins, the words that flowed from her mouth were directed to him. No wonder his regular seat was empty. Harry Dempsey must have been the man with whom Butch was speaking.

"Dempsey." Joey's tone held an edge of fear. "The…uh…dame took a wrong turn."

Harry moved in her direction, his gait slow, deliberate, until he stood within touching distance. "Dame?" That single word rang through the abandoned space.

Oh no. Meggie launched herself from her hiding place and threw her arms about Harry's neck. Locked in his muscular embrace, she rested her chin on his shoulder. His arms tightened around her. "Oh, Harry. I came as fast as I could. Just as we'd planned." The words, she'd intended to carry, came out breathless.

"Fast, huh?" The whisper was against her ear where no one else could hear, raised goose prickles over her entire body. "Guess I'll have to do something about that." He lifted his head. "What are you doing with *my* girl, Joe?"

Joey's hands flew into the air, indicating his surrender. "Sorry, Dempsey. Had no idea she was anyone's quiff—"

Meggie's cheeks burned, and she stiffened at the insult. Harry's one arm gripped her closer. The other shot up, jerking her body like a rag doll. She couldn't see Harry's face with her own now buried in his neck, but she felt the corded muscles contract. A split second later, a sickening crunch sounded followed by a deathlike groan.

Meggie let out her breath and felt a slight shudder ripple through her defender.

"What's going on here?" Butch demanded. "You know this part of the club is off limits, Miss Montley."

Meggie lifted her head from Harry's shoulder and looked into his eyes.

"I requested Lady Margaret's assistance." Harry's gaze never wavered from her.

Meggie voice caught in her throat. She couldn't have spoken to save her life.

"You there," Butch barked. "Drag this piece of shit out back."

Meggie dared a peek and saw Joey Keagan's limp body being hauled out by the arms, legs dragging the ground, by two huge ruffians. She turned back to Harry where a slight sardonic curl lifted his lips.

"Cash or check, doll?" he said.

She swallowed. "W-what?"

He chuckled, setting her cheeks aflame. "A kiss now or later," he said for her ears only.

Meggie wet her lips before answering. "C-check," she stammered out in a husky whisper.

"Check, it is." He loosened his hold, and Meggie slid down his hard body. When her feet touched the floor she realized she still clutched her shoes by the straps.

Harry, tall, deliciously handsome, quietly strong was the most tempting of men. She met those whiskey colored eyes wanting to drown in them.

He set her away from him and stepped back. "Isn't your set about to reconvene, Lady Margaret?" His serious tone belied the twinkle of mischief she was certain she detected.

Meggie started. "Oh, yes. Yes, it is." She backed away, taking in her surroundings. The overhead door open to the club's alley. The large delivery trailer set for loading or unloading, she couldn't discern which. Two more gruff men guarded more barrels as the original two skirted by lugging Joey's unconscious form. Hooch. Heaps of it if she wasn't mistaken.

As she moved into the darkened hall Harry's voice went hard, sending a shiver up her spine. "We need another man, Weaver. Keagan's useless to us now." He flicked his wrist, shaking out his hand that flattened that slime Joey Keagan.

"Yeah, yeah. I'll have someone meet you out back. Tomorrow night. Three A.M."

Meggie cast one last glance to the office where she'd seen all the money stacked on the desk. After shaking her head, she turned and fled the way she'd come.

Harold Evan Dempsey narrowed his eyes on the provocative English miss's exit and groaned. Meggie Montley was up to something. It wasn't Prohibition or Legs Diamond that was likely to kill him. That honor went to the sweetly curvaceous Lady Margaret.

That little maneuver she'd just pulled triggered a desperate need burning through him. He could still feel her breath on his neck, smell the faint scent of roses he'd learned to crave.

Every Friday and Saturday night the past few months when he'd first heard her sing at L'Argent, and now Club 501, he nursed his single whiskey and reveled in the sultry tones that struck something he'd long believed dead, deep in his chest. His lust for her platinum locks and voluptuous body were the reasons behind his bloodshot eyes and worn-out demeanor. And Harry wasn't a man easily led by the head in his pants.

No, it was Meggie Montley's joy for life, that sparkle in her eyes and small smile that made a man forget his father and brother were lost to him forever. Murdered.

Her spare time spent at his table, night after night, teasing him slowly back to life. God, how he wanted her. He wanted her to infuse him with her passion. If he didn't have her soon, he was sure he'd self-combust. Something he knew he'd be a fool to attempt. Harry ran a hand through his hair, frustrated.

How had he wound up appointing himself her personal guardian angel? Devil, more like. But he couldn't seem to help himself from keeping a close eye on the crowd any given night, assuring her safety. But tonight something had gone terribly wrong.

Apparently, he and Frank Markov were due for some words. Joey Keagan shouldn't have even been in the club. The bastard should have been out back, waiting on the arrival of the latest rum shipment. His lip curled involuntarily, and he flexed his hand. The one now sporting torn skin and Keagan's blood. Satisfaction surged through his veins. Keagan was a done deal. If Harry saw him again, he'd probably kill him.

"What the hell was that all about?" Butch demanded.

"Hell, if I know," Harry muttered under his breath.

"Let's get this shit finished up before Markov comes back here demanding answers. And keep your girlfriend out front where she belongs."

Harry couldn't agree more and followed the homely bookkeeper back into the office determined to wrap up the evening's business. Meggie Montley had another set left for the evening's entertainment and Harry had no intention of missing it.

TWO

THE NEXT MORNING MEGGIE stretched and glanced over at Jessie's bed and smiled. It was a jumbled mess as usual. The scent of fresh scones brought her fully awake. Breakfast may come too early in the cramped quarters of the Gables Boardinghouse flat she shared with Jessica, Charli and Eliza, but thank heavens for Charli's bake house dreams.

Eliza. Meggie jumped out of bed and darted for the small kitchen. Charli and Jessie sat at the small round table perusing the *New York World*, each holding their coffee, nibbling on Charli's latest concoction. "Um—" Meggie started.

"Tally ho, Megs. Coffee's on, and Charli's outdone herself. Lemon and basil today." Jess pointed to the tiny counter without lifting her head from the newspaper she was devouring.

"They smell wonderful, Charli. And, Jess, "Tally ho" is a ridiculous word. Remember my Uncle Bartie?"

"Ah, yes. The uncle whose disgusting moose head hung over the hearth. As I recall we managed to deface it one Christmas and barely escaped with our hides intact."

"Yes, that's the one. His favorite greeting was—"

"Tally ho," she and Jess said unanimously. Jess giggled. "You make a good argument."

Meggie reached over the sink and pulled out a cup. "Eliza still sleeping?" She kept the question casual.

Charli glanced up. "No, her bed is made. I'm worried for her. I think she might have a new beau." She frowned. "She shouldn't be staying overnight with him."

Not good news. Damn Eliza for her silly gag order. Armed with coffee, Meggie went to the small, rickety table and sat. "Can we talk?" She tipped a spoon of sugar into her cup.

Jessie looked up quickly. "Is something wrong, Meggie?" Her question drew Charli's attention.

Meggie stared down into her cup. "Yes. I—" She sucked in a deep breath. "I-I'm concerned about my finances."

Jessie laughed. A tinkling, feminine sound that she'd shared their whole life. One that meant she believed nothing bad could happen. Life meant laughter. In the old days, at least. If only that were the case now.

"Is that all?" Jessie shook her head. "Darling." She snatched the section of the paper Charli was reading and flipped to the entertainment section. Slamming it down, she turned it to Meggie with one perfectly manicured nail covering the headline. "*You* are a sensation. Well on your way."

Meggie frowned. "On my way to what?"

Jessie grabbed the paper and read. "A rising new star is on the horizon. Lady Margaret will make your heart weep with those husky, sultry tones of hers. Small appearances in the Broadway productions of *The School of Scandal* and *Betty, Be Good*, have not deterred this deliciously attractive young *lady* from singing gigs around Greater Manhattan. No. These bit-parts Lady Margaret is accruing seem to be serving her needs well. Mark my words, ladies and gents, you would do wise in catching this rising star—if you can."

"Let me see that." Meggie's breath caught and she snatched it back.

"And that's not all," Jessie said smugly. "Paul Whiteman was at Club 501 last night with some new composer. Gershwin something or other."

"Paul Whiteman?" she squeaked.

"Do you know of him?"

"Know him? Know him! They refer to him as the King of Jazz. Dear God. He heard *me*? The man played at Aeolian Hall last year. I heard tell he's receiving five thousand dollars for a single broadcast." She felt faint and fanned herself with the paper. The one small broadcast with Bernie and Edison at WHN had netted her nothing. Of course, she hadn't cared. She was on the radio. But now...she needed money, fast.

"May I have my paper back, please?" Charli shot them a pointed look. Meggie thrust it at her.

"Are you singing tonight?" Jessie asked.

"No. Alyce Kutcher is the featured guest." Meggie rolled her eyes, disgusted.

Jessie laughed. "Don't they refer to her as "The Kitchen"?" Charli covered a fit of giggles behind a string of coughs. "She's awful. How in Hades did she get in with Bernie's little orchestra?"

Meggie snorted. "You have to ask?" She jumped up from the table, knocking her coffee cup askew, barely saving the teetering cup from disaster.

"Careful." Jessie smirked. "See? Soon, you'll be *rolling* in the dough."

They'd strayed way off topic. Like finding Eliza before she turned Dumb Dora on them and went and did some John, *if she hadn't already*. Meggie curled her hand and studied her painted nails. "Where...um...do you suppose Eliza is this early?"

"I'm sure I don't know." Jess, already distracted by her portion of the paper had her head down.

Meggie couldn't very well tell her Eliza didn't have time to wait for Meggie to become a star. She let out a

frustrated sigh. "I'm going to shower. I have errands to run."
Like locating their missing friend.

"Congratulations, Lady Margaret," Charli said.

Meggie dipped a useless curtsey, since neither saw her, and escaped to her room.

Three

THE DREAD IN HARRY'S gut was not new. He pushed open the door to his mother's quaint house in Queens where a mixture of gin and stale cigarettes greeted him. And, thankfully, coffee. He stepped over litter that cluttered the path to the kitchen. "Hey, Ma. Is there enough for me?"

Her smoke-rasped cackle barked in what he decided was a yes then cascaded into an emphysemic fit. "Git me that bottle," she demanded between hacks, pointing to a silver flask next to the stove. Disheveled and frayed gray-hair hid her aged face as she hunched over today's copy of the *World*.

Repressed fury roiled deep in his belly and rose like bile. He pushed it back and snatched up the flask. Vile stuff. Pa's and Lewis's murders had sent her spiraling into oblivion. His idea bank in helping Ma was depleted. The grip on his own control was taut.

"What are you reading, Ma?" He set the bottle on the table. He snatched up her cup and turned to fill both.

She pulled a long swig from the flask and let out a satisfied sigh. A crooked index finger tapped the paper. "That shoulda' been me," she huffed. "I was at the top of my game 'fore yer daddy stole my career."

Harry set fresh coffee in front of her and leaned in to see what she was rattling on about. The first few words had him biting back a groan. *A rising new star is on the horizon. Lady Margaret...*

"I thought you were happy, Ma," Harry said quietly.

But she was on her rant, and there was nothing that could stop her. "I coulda' been a star. I was on the brink." Tears filled her eyes. He left us destitute. Destitute, I tell ya."

Her tears always did him in. Harry turned away.

He didn't need a reminder that Meggie Montley was on the brink of taking the world by storm. He'd known it the first time he'd heard her sing. When her voice transitioned into that seductive contralto, it was like she'd melded through to his bones...his soul.

He had no business fantasizing about her. He was a business owner out for justice, and she was young, about to hit her prime. Disgusted at the constant unrealistic fantasies, he flipped on the faucet surprised at the slight tremble in his hand.

Determined to shove away such distraction, he concentrated on the matter at hand and surveyed the tiny kitchen. Dishes covered the sink and countertops. He hadn't been home in two weeks. "Ma, when's the last time you ate, huh?"

"Yesterday."

Yesterday. He snatched up a dish towel, went to the back porch and opened the icebox. The ice had long since melted. He pulled out a jug of milk and sniffed. The sour odor hit his nose with a vengeance. He jerked his head back, banging it against the doorframe. Moldy cheese and some kind of vegetable he couldn't make out were the only other items in the box. *Hell.*

"Yoo whoo."

Harry glanced up. Dixie—or doxy as he'd never been able to resist referring to her—Ward lifted one hand in greeting and started across the yard. Her short, bright red hair was plastered in waves against her head, full hips squeezed into a tight skirt, generous breasts bouncing, unconfined. The woman had less subtlety than the lighted signs on Broadway.

"Hello, Harry. How is that sweet mama of yours today?" She held up a covered dish. "I brought her some lunch."

"Much thanks, Dox—er, Miss Ward." Her anxiousness in asking after his ma was suspect. He doubted she'd been by since the last time he'd made it home. He swallowed a muttered oath. It wasn't Doxy's place to feed Ma. "Would you care for coffee?"

"Oh, that sounds lovely." One of those large breasts brushed his arm. It did nothing for him. Just sent his thoughts spiraling to Margaret Montley and that red dress she'd performed in the night before. How she'd clung to him in the darkened depths of Club 501, breaths rapid and unsteady when she'd thrown herself in his arms. Then slid down his body, reminding him just how long it had been since he'd been with a woman.

Shaking his head, he stepped back, allowing Doxy through the door.

"Hello, Dixie," Ma said. "I see you done cornered Harry." Dixie's face turned as red as her hair which sent his mother into another fit of hacks.

Harry got her some water and set it on the table, retrieving the flask at the same time. He glanced at her coffee. Full. "Ma. Miss Ward brought you lunch."

His mother, wisely, said nothing. She rose from the table and went through to the living room.

Doxy, however, planted herself at the table, preparing for a long visit it appeared, and glanced over the paper. Harry ignored her and started on the dishes.

"We miss you around these parts, Harry." Her husky tones told him exactly what she missed. He and Dixie had had a thing way back. Years, back.

He just grunted.

"Oh, Harry." Her shrill laugh sounded like rusty nails on a sheet of metal.

"Been pretty busy with the marina since Pa and Lewis..." His voice trailed.

It took damn near an hour to get Doxy-Dixie to leave. Harry made a trip to the market, loaded up the ice box with fresh ice, and fixed Ma a few meals to last her a couple of days. Two weeks was too long between visits home.

He woke her from a long nap and sat at the table, making her eat at least half of what he'd put on her plate. Still, Lady Margaret devoured every thought. With an index finger he slid the *World* over and, unable to resist, read the article that spelled out reason after reason why Harry should stay far, far away from Lady Margaret Montley.

She wasn't singing that night, but on her off nights, she occasionally showed up at Club 501 with her friend Jessica Hatton.

Thirty minutes later, Harry was back on the subway bound for Manhattan.

Four

MEGGIE SWIPED THE FINISHING touch of paint across her lips then checked her appearance in the full length glass on the back of the bathroom door. Her knee-length dress of black crepe, accentuated her waistline perfectly. She abhorred those sacks the flappers were wearing these days. She spun in a circle then drifted into the kitchenette where the entertainment section of the newspaper still lay open to the article depicting her future. She picked it up, smiling. But worry for Eliza seeped in and she dropped the paper.

Eliza hadn't returned to the flat before Charli left for her shift at Club 501 hours ago, and Jessie was off scooping the lead for her next big story. Meggie shuddered, praying Eliza didn't end up found hidden somewhere in a clump of debris no better than tossed out garbage like Roxy.

Blast it, where *was* Eliza? She hadn't been accounted for all day. Meggie had tried searching for her near the sewing factory, then the coffee shop where the four sometimes met on the rare occasion their schedules allowed. Meggie glanced at the wall clock in the kitchen. Nine o'clock.

Waiting around an empty flat for Eliza was doing no one any good. She grabbed her used ermine wrap and matching clutch then darted out the door just in time to see the backside of the Trolley whipping around the corner. She let out a frustrated sigh. The evening was balmy enough for her six block walk. She just didn't fancy the streets off Broadway where there were very few street lamps. Any tiny noise made her jump reminding her of Roxy's unfortunate end.

A block from Club 501 Meggie caught sight of a tall attractive man assisting Eliza from a newer Model T. Meggie sagged, relieved. He gripped her friend by the chin and planted a facer on her. How exciting! Eliza *did* have a new beau. Everything was fine. In the morning, Eliza would downplay her romantic adventures between the four of them over fresh baked scones and coffee.

Meggie started forward. The man grinded himself against Eliza—in plain sight of anyone, then grabbed her breast and squeezed. Meggie froze as he kissed her again, hard, before striding to the driver's side of the auto. He climbed in, slammed the door and drove off without so much as a wave in Eliza's direction.

How could Eliza allow him to treat her like that on the street like a common...common harlot...or—

Eliza wiped her mouth with her forearm, her eyes wild.

"Eliza," Meggie called out.

Eliza spun.

"*He's* not your new beau, is he?" Meggie demanded.

Tears filled Eliza's eyes. She stood stock-still, hands clenched at her side.

"Tell me," Meggie pleaded. "I wish to help. But I can't if you aren't honest with me."

"I don't know what to do," Eliza cried. "I promised my mum."

"Promised your mum what?"

"That I wouldn't be any man's—" She choked, unable to finish.

"You aren't." Meggie took her by the arms and shook her. She pulled in a deep breath.

Eliza shrugged from Meggie's hold, drew her shoulders back and looked around, before meeting Meggie's gaze. "What am I to do?" Her voice was low and shaking. "A thousand dollars is an impossible amount."

Meggie swallowed. That was indeed a fortune. She reached again for one of Eliza's fisted hands. "I'll...uh, admit the cost is astronomical. But surely there's a way. Between Jessie, Charli and I—"

Eliza jerked her hands away. "No! You mustn't tell anyone. You promised me, Meggie."

"But Eliza—"

"No! No. I'll work this out on my own." Eliza turned and disappeared down the stone stairs to the entrance of the club, an ominous silence filling the atmosphere with her departure.

"How, Eliza?" Meggie whispered to the night air. *One thousand dollars.* How on earth could they come up with that kind of blunt? The thought crossed her mind to contact Sam, but she tossed that away just as quickly. Sam would certainly have helped before but Papa's death had turned her eldest brother into a stodgy old man by the day of the funeral. Lady Hatton would help. She was always generous, always willing to assist those less fortunate. But Lady Hatton posed two problems. The fact of the matter was that Jess, Charli and Meggie had run away, and Lady Hatton was sure to tell Meggie's own mother. More importantly, if Eliza caught wind of Meggie going to Jessie's mother, Eliza might choose to disappear.

Meggie turned in a slow circle at a loss. There must be *something* she could do to raise some money. Damn, Eliza's silly promise in not letting Meggie ask for help. Stacks and stacks of crates flashed through her mind, followed by the stacks of cash Butch had been counting. There must be lots of money to be made. But how? How could she, a mere woman—*Wait*. Wasn't Butch sending someone to help Harry with a shipment of illegal liquor?

She had friends. Lots of friends. Actor friends, costume friends, *make-up artist friends*. Eliza might keep her from telling anyone the real issue, but there were other ways to get help. Meggie spun around and marched down the street. Straight to Broadway.

Harry leaned against the wall near his regular table, one arm folded across his chest and sipped at his single whiskey, glaring at Theodore Clifford. Someone should shoot the bastard for some of the items the man stretched the truth for in his sensationalistic approach to news story-writing.

Harry glanced at his watch, disappointed. Eleven-thirty, and no sign of Meggie Montley. He'd caught sight of one of her roommates over an hour ago. She'd looked upset, but Vince Taggart swooped in and Harry turned his attention back to the entertainment. Alyce Kutcher. The woman had nothing on Lady Margaret. He tuned her out, morosely, watching newcomers stream in. Once the theaters let out, there wouldn't an inch in the place to maneuver about. The joint would be packed despite its size.

"Hey, Harry." The come-hither pitch could barely be heard above the hum of the crowd.

"Alyce." He nodded once in her direction.

"I finish up at one. What do you say we meet right after?"

Harry's gaze roved over her short dark, wavy hair, to blood red lips that were too thin for his tastes. A myriad of necklaces were draped around her neck designed to draw the eye to an impressive cleavage. He lifted his drink and sipped. "I'm working, doll. Sorry."

She leaned in, and her voice dipped into a husky timbre. "Then how about you and me for ten minutes? Care to meet in the Green Room?"

He couldn't help it. He laughed and shook his head. The Kitchen never did understand the word no.

Five

"WHAT DO YOU THINK, Georgie? Will I pass?" Meggie stared at her reflection in the mirror, stunned by the transformation. She wrinkled her nose. "This mustache tickles. How do men stand it?"

Georgie, a tall, slender make-up artist she knew from *Betty, Be Good* at *The Globe,* wore his black hair slicked back. "It's a sign of masculinity, dear. Besides it's the best way to hide your delicate features. It's not easy turning a beautiful, rising star into a bootlegging thug. Now, stand still. Are the bindings too tight?"

"Unbearable," she muttered, feeling the heat crawl up her neck.

"Don't worry. As soon as I adjust the suspenders, we'll add a jacket. Just don't take it off. Anyone with eyes could spot there's more there than should be for a young, thin man." Georgie turned her and adjusted the straps that were designed to hold up her knickers.

"These trousers seem a bit short," she said.

"That's the style. The boys are quite proud of their silly argyle socks." He spun her about again and knotted the necktie.

Meggie slipped on the jacket then studied the overall package in the mirror.

"Really, darling, we should cut your hair." She watched him eye the smoothed back version tied at the nape of her neck with anticipation.

"Forget it. It's bad enough that we put this brown rinse on it. You're certain it will wash out after a day or two?" Her voice trembled.

Georgie chuckled. "Don't cry. That emasculates the entire picture of what we are trying to portray." He grabbed her hand then frowned. "We'll have to cut your nails."

Meggie groaned. "Gloves. I'll wear gloves." From the corner of her eye, she caught the time on Georgie's desk clock. "Good heavens, is that right?"

"Two fifteen? I'm afraid so, love." He held out a pageboy cap and a pair of brown gloves.

"Blast." She snatched both items from him. "I've got to go."

With a quick hug, Meggie scrambled out the door. After a colossal failure at flagging down a cab she began the brisk walk to Club 501, running over the conversation between Harry and Butch the night before.

The truck was scheduled for three A.M, which should give her plenty of time to get to the alley and hang back. *The alley in which Roxy was found, dead.* She didn't know what she would do if Joey's replacement beat her there. Bopping him on the head was an option, she supposed, scanning the ground for weapon. *Weapon.* She needed a weapon. This hair-brained scheme was certain to get her killed. If not this one, the next. How did she keep ending up in these foolish situations time and again?

Shadows loomed, and every so often a match struck, and the red-tipped glow of a cigarette illuminated a face. Meggie pulled a deep breath to steady her jumpy nerves. Adapted her mind into her stage persona mode. Forced a casual stride. It occurred and surprised her in how comfortable the oxford-styled uppers were compared to the toe-choking heels she wore nightly. She shoved her hands deep into the pockets of her tweed coat.

The closer she grew to Club 501 the tighter her stomach knotted. She reached the block and crept around the building, nerves taut as the gory details relayed by Jess and Charli in her head like the film with Ramon Navarro she and Jess had seen. Only the scene in her head appeared in vivid colors. The most dominant being red.

Fingers clenched to stop their trembling, she hugged the side of the building. Nothing.

She didn't know whether to be relieved or furious after all of her and Georgie's painstaking efforts.

Just as she let out a dejected sigh, a truck rolled in with the lights cut. Meggie sank to the ground behind a row of bushes and watched. An overhead door to Club 501 raised and Butch hurried out, Harry following in his more deliberate gait. A hundred bats flew into motion deep within her abdomen. Could she do this? *Eliza. Eliza needs help.*

Meggie was an actress, wasn't she? An accomplished actress. Newspaper articles attested her acclaim, and this was her most important role to date. Rising to her feet, she squared her shoulders.

"Where the fuck is he?" Harry demanded. Meggie fought an urge to run the opposite direction. "We need another man."

"He'll be here. He'll be here," Butch snapped.

"What the hell is his name?"

Butch barked out a laugh. "What the hell's wrong with you, Harry? I've never seen you this out of sorts. Ah, need a boff, do ya? I saw you talking to Alyce. I'm pretty sure—"

Meggie cringed. Did Harry have a thing for "The Kitchen"?

"That's enough," Harry growled. "His name."

"Sid. Flash is sending him over. Keep an eye out for him, I'll be in the office if you need me." Butch slipped inside.

This was it. Now or never. Meggie pulled her cap down over her brow and stepped from her hidden place among the bushes.

"Sid? 'Bout damn time," Harry said. "Let's go."

With a steady pace, Meggie edged her way to Harry, knees threatening to give way. Harry's mood kept her quiet and watchful. With the grace of mountain lion, he leaped up in the bed of the truck. Her first real attack of fear slammed her when she gaged the height at which she'd need to somehow maneuver *and* appear masculine. She stole a glance at Harry who watched her, with curled lips. She threw out a gloved hand. The curled lip shifted to a disgusted smirk, but with a grunt he hauled her up. Just like the Harry she believed him to be.

He banged on the ceiling and the truck jerked into motion, tossing her to the straw covered floor.

LIGHTWEIGHT. HARRY TURNED HIS gaze out to the street. The boy couldn't have been more than sixteen, though that mustache was pretty full for one so young and slight. "You been doing this long, Sid?" His shirt was too damned white.

The kid just grunted, leaned back and pulled his cap further over his face.

Harry decided to do the same. No sense wasting unnecessary words. These weren't the assignments where a man made lifelong friends. Pelham was an hour's drive. They'd catch the boat out to the Long Island Sound. Hell, he'd be lucky to make it home by six.

The depth of night meant less traffic and faster time. The usual sixty minute trek took forty-five. The truck lurched to a stop and Harry jumped out. The kid attempted the same, barely avoiding a conk on his head but for Harry's grab on his arm. The maneuver sent his cap flailing. Jesus, the kid needed food, he had no muscle.

Harry narrowed his eyes on the brown, lackluster hair tied back with a black strap. Sid jerked his arm from Harry's hold and swooped his cap from the ground.

A whiff of something vaguely familiar—soft and floral, flowers of the hothouse variety, tingled his nostrils. A not-so-good feeling started deep in Harry's gut. The kid jammed his cap on his head, stepping back. *Roses.*

"Meggie," he whispered harshly.

The kid whipped his head around, facing him, mustache slightly off center. Angled like the Leaning Tower of Pisa.

"What the fu—" He stopped himself from letting his vulgar language touch such delicate ears.

"Boat's ready for you, cap'n."

Harry jerked ramrod straight. "Give us a minute, Marco."

"Sure thing, cap'n, but time's a wastin', they won't give you too long. You know the score."

"Yeah, yeah. I said a minute," he growled. He turned back to his companion, fury surging through his veins. "What the hell do you think you're doing?" He kept his voice to a whisper. The danger temperature just hit the hundred mark.

Her brilliant eyes flashed. "I need blunt. And this seemed the quickest way to obtain it." Her clipped British accent was low but definitely the same distinct voice that haunted his dreams night after night.

"The butt of a cigar? What the hell are you talking about?" The effort to keep his voice low was building the pressure in his skull.

"Money. Cash. Currency," she said just as hotly.

"For what!"

"For—" she stopped, mouth gaping. It snapped shut. "Never you mind—*cap'n*—I-I have my reasons."

"I'll give you the god damned money. How much?" He glanced over his shoulder.

A figure stood on the bow of the boat. "What's the hold up, cap'n? Time's a'wastin'."

She followed his gaze. "One thousand dollars."

"One thous—are you out of your fuc—" Harry pulled himself up. "What the hell for?"

"Keep your voice down." She raised herself up. She looked magnificent, despite the crooked mustache. Only where the hell were her curves?

"What for?"

Her gaze dropped to her feet. "I can't say."

"God almighty. Do you know what kind of people these are? What kind of danger you're putting yourself in? *Me* in?"

That jerked her head up.

"These men don't give a shit whether you are the biggest star on the Silver Screen or the lowest life in the subway."

"I-I'm sorry." Tears glinted on her lashes.

"Oh, for God's sake. You'll damn sure give us away if you blubber like a girl." He squinted out in dark. "I can't very well leave you here. You'll have to come with me." He rested his gaze back on her. "Keep that hat low on your head and don't say a fucking word. If they kill me, you can bet when they find your body there won't be anything recognizable." He felt like an ass letting the curse words fly. But if something happened to her—it didn't bear thinking about. Then, to see her lips tremble. *Hell.* "I don't suppose you know how to use a gun."

"I-I used one on stage once," she whispered.

Compressing his lips, he tugged the Luger from his trousers at his lower back, hidden beneath his jacket. "Damn thing's loaded." He grabbed her hand, its utter femininity reaching through her glove. How had he missed that when he'd hauled her into the truck? He was an idiot.

Shoving away fear that centered deep within his belly, he positioned the gun in her hand, showing her the proper hold. "If you have to shoot, try to aim it in someone else's direction. Stay behind me."

He let out a held breath at her shaky nod.

"Let's go. And straighten the mustache."

Six

MEGGIE STARED AT THE heavy metal in her hand, feet rooted to the ground, shock coursing through her.

"Sid!"

Harry's fierce bark startled her forward. Was she supposed to hold it? Put it in her pocket? Stuff it in her pants like Harry had? She shoved the gun in her pocket, carefully keeping it pointed to the ground, and hurried her steps.

The moon was but a sliver in the night sky, only offering up the others in shadowed depths. She darted after him, staying close on his heels. Her fingers moved to the hair above her itchy lip and pressed the piece firmly in place.

"Where's Keaton?" The gruff growl pierced the night.

Harry's sudden stop caught Meggie by surprise, and she plowed right into him. He responded with a chuckle that sounded more like an evil menace. "Indisposed." He jerked Meggie by the scruff of her jacket, pulling her from behind him. "This here's, Sid." He shot her a flat grin. "He's mute."

Mute? She glared at him. Not that it affected him. He'd switched his attention back to the figure in the boat.

A long pause ensued and Meggie felt the weight of the man's stare. "We ain't got all night."

Harry strode down the pier and jumped in a boat no larger than the loo Meggie and her flatmates shared with their neighbors at the Gables Boardinghouse. Every feminine sensibility she possessed was offended by Harry's actions from stomping off ahead of her to his crude language. His head dipped from sight and a flutter of panic pulsed through her veins.

"Come on, Sid," he taunted. "I'll help you in. This is the kid's first time on a boat," he directed to his companion.

Meggie gritted her teeth. This was *not* her first time on a boat. What of her trans-Atlantic crossing on the *Empress of India*, just six months ago? Besides, that thing he'd just boarded could not be considered a boat.

Oh. He said he'd help her. She ran forward; he was so clever.

WHERE'D YOU FIND THIS green boy, cap'n? If'n he's worth his weight in gold, we're in trouble." The cigarette in Marco's mouth bobbed around the words, yet surprisingly the fag never fell. Just the ashes. He stood at the back near the motor, his hands at his hips.

"Keagan landed himself in some trouble. Lay off Sid," Harry said. "We gotta job to do." *Like find Legs Diamond and put a bullet in him, and keep Meggie Montley from getting them all killed.*

Harry moved to the side, hoping he blocked Marco's view. How the woman thought anyone would believe her a man was beyond him. Despite the masculine attire, she was one hundred percent woman. One who'd filled his dreams since the first night she'd taken the stage at Club 501. His vision conjured up the sultry moves as he'd seen her sway to soft percussions that filled the air, eyes closed. Once her voice let loose, the sweetest sound touched him, making him almost believe there was a heaven.

If they got out of this alive, he promised himself, he would take a kiss from those full lips once and for all.

Meggie reached the boat and Harry stepped back, clenching his hands into fists. Grabbing her by the waist would be a dead giveaway to her gender. If Marco realized she was a woman, what was to stop him from pulling out a gun and shooting Harry in the back, or both of them for that matter? He didn't trust Marco any more than he did the bastard who'd killed his father and brother.

"Hurry it up, cap'n. They won't wait all night."

Meggie's feet had no more than touched the boat before Marco gunned the engine, throwing her into Harry. He landed on his ass, her on his lap. A small squeal erupted from her. Harry glanced quickly at Marco. Harry set her aside. "Hold on to your hat, boy."

She glared at him but a gloved hand plastered the hat against her head, drawing his chuckle.

Between the wind and the motor, neither Harry nor Marco were inclined to speak. Just as well, as Harry couldn't conceive of any idea in how to keep Meggie safe. God damn, Diamond was supposed to be on the big boat. This was the opportunity he'd been waiting for. Take the bastard out, feed the fish in the Sound. He flicked a look in her direction—no way could he take the chance on her getting hurt. A vice squeezed deep inside his chest, making it difficult to breathe.

The night air on the boat in early November was cold, and everything he'd fantasized about Lady Margaret Montley seemed to fall in line. Her quick assessment of the danger they faced to the lack of complaining of the frigid weather most likely chapping her lovely nose and cheeks. Everything about her sang to his dark soul. *Everything* except the idiocy of dressing like a man and traipsing about the city in the middle of the night, that is. Which begged the question again—why? Why the hell did she need that much money? Christ, what a poser. An unmitigated disaster.

"Up ahead, cap'n." Marco's thick accent barely sounded over the motor.

The engine cut, jarring him back. In the distance ahead, a shadowed vessel sat low in the water with at least two masts. It was long and dark. From this distance Harry couldn't see anyone aboard, but he knew they were watching for him. He glanced out at the black night, but with Meggie in the boat the last thing he needed, or wanted, was gunfire.

Once the boat was drifting, the wind died down. But the November air was biting. Water slapped the skiff, rocking it gently.

"That you, cap'n?" The voice came from the schooner, echoing in the night.

"Who else you expecting?" Harry called back.

"Come on up, then."

Harry glanced at Marco over his shoulder and gave him a sharp nod. Marco cranked up the motor and guided them around the bow. Harry leaned over to Meggie, fear clawing at him. "How you doing, Sid?"

She looked at him, eyes-wide. She hid her emotions well, and thankfully, kept to the "mute" story. Her eyes flashed to Marco then back to his. He took her one blink as a sign, and moved away.

Dread weighted, as deep as a block of iron, in his gut. He latched onto the roped ladder and climbed aboard the schooner, straight into the pit of vipers waiting, and tossed another useless glance over his shoulder in the depth of the night.

At the top rung a pair of stout hands hauled him up and over. Harry caught himself before he stumbled to his knees. The deck was dotted with a few lanterns for light, but not many.

"Who's in the boat, Harry?"

"Marco and Sid.

Legs Diamond stepped into view, his light color fedora low on his forehead, expression stoic and cold. "Heard Keagan got the shit beat out of him."

"Damn sure did. Bastard messed with the wrong girl." Harry savored that tidbit.

Legs chuckled. "You liked to have killed him, Harry."

Keagan slid into sight behind the savvy gangster. *Ah, shit.* Too late. Harry fell into the trap like a starving kitten going for food. So the bastard had been working for Legs all along.

"Yeah, you dick, and now it's my turn to repay the favor." He laughed. "And then I'll go back for the quiff."

Harry started toward Keagan pleased with another opportunity to beat the shit out of the weasel. Maybe this time he'd finish the job.

Legs laughed again. A malicious menace that filled the Long Island Sound. "Not so fast." He jerked his head to the bulkhead. "You remember Alphonse Milano, don't you, Harry? Perhaps better known as Shaky-hand Alphonse?"

Alphonse lumbered into the meager light, dragging a ragamuffin of a figure by the collar. Yeah, Harry remembered him and his gut tightened at the sight. No lips, large nose, ears sticking out so far from his head, if the wind caught he'd catch flight and drop in the Sound. Shaky-hand Alphonse—the bastard who'd killed his father and brother. A numbing sensation started at the base of Harry's neck and wrapped his brain.

Alphonse tossed the slight figure at Harry's feet.

"Harry." His eyes were swollen shut. Bruises covered his face to unrecognizable, one hand missing two fingers, the remaining fingers deformed, bones broken. Yet, the voice. A most recognizable voice. "It's me, Harry."

"Lewis." Raging fire surged through Harry, shoving out the surrealism, choking him along with the shock learning his brother wasn't dead after all. Harry jerked the Luger from the position at his lower back and fired. Alphonse dropped to the deck in a heap.

"Ah, now, Harry, why'd you have to go and do that?" Legs clucked his tongue.

Harry pointed the gun at Legs then swung it towards Keagan. "You next?"

Keagan's hands flew to the air as he backed away, fading into the night.

"Throw down your gun." Harry aimed his words at Keagan but his focus was on Legs from his peripheral vision.

"I ain't got a piece, Dempsey. I swear." Keagan was a begging weasel.

Legs arm came up, extending a tommy. "Ho, shit." Damn thing must have weighed some twelve pounds. Harry threw his body over Lewis, firing off a round at the same time. The machine gun's rapid shots flew wild over Harry's head, stopping as quickly as they'd begun, as the Tommy thudded on the deck. Silence filled the air. Harry jumped to his feet, threw Lewis over his shoulder and backed to the bulwark, Luger pointed out. Legs lay still, slumped over his gun, and where ever Keagan had slithered to, Harry refused to contemplate.

"Marco, catch," Harry called out softly and dropped Lewis into the skiff below. A soft grunt met his ears and he leaped over after him. His landing rocked the boat hard enough that water sloshed in. "Hit it, Marco."

The engine roared to life, the noise deafening in the cold night air. An unconscious Lewis lay in the muck and Harry touched his fingers to the pulse at his neck. It was faint, but there.

Meggie shifted over and lifted Lewis's head to her lap. Harry met widened-eyes that reflected the sliver of moonlight. Her bottom lip trembled and he resisted reaching over to squeeze her hand.

Emotions suffocated him, stabbing him from every direction. He scrubbed a hand over his face, stuffed them back. So much could still go wrong, and now he had two fragile lives to guard. He looked to the heavens. *My hands aren't big enough.*

The engine cut, snapping Harry to the situation at hand. They were halfway between the schooner and shore.

Silence, once again, roared in the night. Harry narrowed his eyes on the old man.

A portable, lantern-style flashlight burned to life next to Marco. He struck a match, lighting the cigarette that appeared permeated to his lip. He tossed the match overboard and sucked deep, then blew out a stream of white smoke. "Well, cap'n. Guess there ain't to be no cabbage fer us tonight."

"I guess not, Marco. Sorry."

"Dammit all to hell. My moll won't be happy."

"You know there's more to be had, Marco. Plenty of trouble boys to hang with if you want easy dough."

"What!" Meggie gasped. "We aren't to be paid? At all?"

Marco froze, shock painting his scraggily features. His gaze darted to Meggie's sitting form. Harry swallowed a groan.

"Huh. You ain't so mute then after all." The faint light beamed off a pistol in Marco's hand. His arm moved slowly and stopped, pointed at Harry.

FEAR STOPPED MEGGIE'S HEART, the breath caught in her throat. Why did she always have to open her mouth at the wrong time?

"Put the gun away, Marco. This here's Lady Margaret Montley."

Meggie lifted her chin. "I sing with the Bernie-Edison Orchestra."

Marco chuckled, the gun never wavering in his hand. "Who's ta stop me from killing you, cap'n, and makin' a bit of a profit off yer *Lady* Margaret Munt…Munt…whatever her name is? Why, I could sell her off and make double what I should'a took ta'night."

Terrified, Meggie slipped a trembling hand in the pocket of her jacket and wrapped her fingers around the gun Harry slipped to her earlier.

"No one, I venture to say, cap'n. Now, drop yer piece over the side. Real nice an' slow like." Harry hesitated and Marco raised the gun.

Fingers shaking uncontrollably, Meggie raised her gun in his direction. "No." Her voice cracked. She forced an impossible calm. "No," she said again.

"I said, drop it, cap'n."

"I'll shoot. I-I will." But she feared her trembling endangered Harry's life. The man whose head rested in her lap stirred. His hand slipped over hers, fingers lining hers, and squeezed. The gun went off, jolting her whole arm, ringing her ears. She screamed, dropping the hot metal and slumped back.

In an instant Harry had her wrapped in his embrace. "Meggie." She burrowed deeper, shaking uncontrollably.

"It's okay, sweetheart. You had no other option."

Meggie clung his warmth, his voice.

"She didn't do it, Harry. I had to do something to keep her from killing one of us." The raspy tones indicated a distinct lack of use.

"Are you all right? Meggie?"

She made an effort to pull herself together. She straightened out of his hold. "Yes. Yes."

He took her chin and lifted it. Forced her to gaze to his. "Don't worry, the worst is over now, Lady Margaret." He spoke softly. "I need to take care of that bag of bones. Are you sure you're okay?"

With a deep breath, Meggie nodded.

Harry made his way to the back of the skiff and bent over Marco. "He's not dead." He went to the seat near the engine, lifted the cushion and pulled out a rope. "Well, Marco, you fucked with the wrong man." He laughed. "And the wrong woman."

"This is quite a dame you've got, Harry."

Shock held Meggie silent. The words in her head refused to form into any sort of coherent sense. Like 'who was this man too weak to sit? How did Harry know him?' And 'how had *she* shot a man?'

"I think I'm going to be ill." She launched herself to the side of the boat, flinging the man from her lap, uncaring that his head landed hard on the boat's bottom. A second later not a thing was left in her already empty stomach. A large hand smoothed the hair from her brow, the tie holding it back long gone. Tears filled her eyes. She couldn't face Harry's wrath, though she deserved it, every last word. But his set down would do her in.

"Are you crying, Lady Margaret?" She was trying not to, but his gentle question sent the tears spilling over.

She shook her head. But he had to know she lied, as certainly her training as an actress hadn't granted her such skills.

He chuckled softly, which only added to her emotional outburst.

"Here, sweetheart. Take a sip of this." He took her head and held a small flask to her lips. "It will help with the shock. Dispel that nasty taste from your mouth."

With a small nod, Meggie accepted the peace offering and took a healthy swig. It burned all the way down her throat. Another bout of tears surfaced. "Where did that come from?" she coughed out between words.

"Marco has a pretty dependable stash hidden. I just happen to know his hiding places. This stuff will kill damn near anything."

"Who's your friend?" she said once she caught her breath.

"My once-thought-dead brother, Lewis. Lewis, meet Lady Margaret Montley."

She glanced over her shoulder to the man.

"Ma'am. The pleasure is mine."

He was a charmer.

"You all right, now?" He spoke against her ear.

Meggie inhaled carefully then nodded.

After squeezing her hand, Harry moved to the back of the boat, kicking Marco's feet out of his way. "There's coppers crawling all over Pelham Bay. We'll turn Marco over to them. Someone should be able to give us a lift back to the city. We need a croaker to give you the once over, Lewis." He flashed the light three times then fired up the engine.

The cold air against Meggie's face did much for her constitution and she shifted back to Lewis and leaned over him. "I'm sorry about your head, Mr. Dempsey. Can you explain what a 'croaker' is?"

A groused laugh erupted from him, followed by a short groan. "The doc. Lady Margaret—*the* Lady Margaret? The one from the radio? WHN?"

"Well, yes, I suppose that's so. We did do a broadcast early on, once I'd joined Bernie's."

"How the hell—er, pardon, Miss Montley. Jeepers—how, uh, did you hook up with my bluenose brother?"

Meggie frowned. "Bluenose?"

"Killjoy. Harry's not the greatest fun to be had."

She cast a glance over her shoulder at Harry who steered the motor with his large efficient, most capable hands. "I beg to differ, Mr. Dempsey. Harry is the furthest thing from a killjoy I know of."

"Please, Miss Montley. I'm on my back here. Might you call me Lewis?"

The first real grin of the night touched her. "I'm happy to make your acquaintance, Lewis. And I insist you call me Meggie. May I assist you up?"

"I'd be right grateful, Meggie."

She slipped an arm beneath the thin shoulders and lifted him. He weighed but a feather. "What happened up on that bigger boat?"

"I think my killjoy brother offed one of the most famous bootleggers of the decade. Did you kill the bastard, Harry?"

"I don't know."

"I don't understand," Meggie said. "I thought we were just supposed to pick up a shipment of...of..." She threw out a hand. Blast. She hadn't any idea what they were supposed to have bootlegged which was obviously nothing now. Thoughts of Eliza engulfed her. She'd failed her friend. Utterly and completely. And now they weren't to be paid.

"Gentleman Jack ain't no gentleman, cap'n. He'll come after you," Marco piped up.

The old man's voice startled her, his words stirring confusion along with the thread of unease through her. "Who is this Gentleman Jack? And if he is a gentleman, why would he come after Harry?" Meggie's head began to throb with all the innuendoes.

"Gentleman Jack is another name Legs Diamond is well-known by," Lewis told her. "I don't know where they came up with the name "Gentleman" for the bastard, but he got the name "Legs" for flaunting his money and...uh...er…women all over town. Hell, all over New York for that matter."

She glanced back at Harry, concerned. "Will this "gentleman" try to hurt Harry?" Meggie couldn't imagine singing at Club 501 without Harry sitting in his usual corner. Without those dark, fathomless eyes pinned on her. He brought out a side of her she'd never realized existed.

She snapped her gaze back to Lewis's harsh laugh. "Oh, yeah. He's likely to cut off his ba—er, pardon my French, Miss Montley, Meggie. I forget myself."

Meggie should have been mortified. Instead, fury raged through her. "Why should this Legs-Gentleman want to-to—" She couldn't form the phrase.

"He murdered our pa. And by the look I saw on my brother's face, he thought Legs had done killed me too." Lewis leaned against the side of the skiff and closed his eyes, exhaustion seeming to have claimed him. "As it turns out, he only wounded me a little, and starved me a lot. Damn, I'm hungry."

Seven

THE RELIEF THAT SPILLED through Harry in finding Lewis alive and delivering Margaret Montley home safe was overwhelming. The wait to get Lewis home to Ma left Harry fantasizing he possessed some magic artifact he could rub for three wishes. Wish number 1: Lewis's health, of course. Nothing could dim the joy in Harry's heart than seeing his brother hadn't perished at the hands of Legs Diamond via Shaky-Alphonse. Wish number 2: Ma's elation so complete at having her younger son back, her craving for bathtub gin quashed forever. The shit was poison. Wish number 3—Harry's gaze flew to Lady Margaret and he took a deep breath—Wish number 3:Stealing the blinding smile she turned on Lewis, to keep for Harry, and Harry alone.

What a pipe dream. Meggie Montley could never belong to just Harry. Not with her talent, and the momentum of that talent. The lady's career was on the verge of exploding, and no way in hell would Harry be the one to hold her back.

He squinted behind him into the inky night. The faint shadow of the lighthouse guard was moving in on the schooner. Harry let out a relieved breath. One step closer to getting Lewis and Meggie out of danger. He glanced toward the woman who kept his dreams captive. Any ordered semblance of her previously contained hair had long since dissipated.

"What are you planning on do with me, cap'n?"

Harry tore his gaze from the locks whipping across Meggie's face and focused. "I ought to drop you in the Sound. That hunk of metal lodged in your chest in place of a heart would drag you straight to the bottom. You could feed the marine life for weeks."

"Ah, cap'n. I wouldn'na shot you." The man put whining babies to shame.

"Shut it, Marco." Lights dotted the shoreline. He counted at least twelve. He lifted the flashlight and signaled the coast. A few minutes later he dropped the engine into a lower gear. "Sid," he barked. A nudge of pleasure shot through him watching her gaze shoot to him. "Get that hat on and grab the rope. Toss it up on the dock when I give the word." He bit back a laugh at her scowl but inordinately pleased that she did as he asked. She slammed her newsboy cap on her head as he guided the boat alongside the dock. "Now," he said.

On the first try the rope slid back into the boat, but she snatched it up and threw over a second time with an aggravated force. "Mute time," he told her, dragging Marco with him. He stood him nearby before hoisting Lewis up carefully. He moved to the ladder. "Hey, Warren. Got some good news. Shaky-Alphonse is dead."

"Good job, Harry."

"But my brother, Lewis here, he needs medical attention. You got someone who can get us to the city, fast like?"

"Of course."

After handing Lewis up, Harry hauled Meggie, none too gently, to the ladder. Unable to help himself, his fingers molded her waist and he lifted her halfway up. She scrambled from his hold much too soon. "This is Sid. He's mute."

"He ain't mute," Marco yelled out. "He's a she. Some big-time, famous singer—"

Harry's fist shot out. Marco's slight figure crumpled like a rag doll. Harry tossed him to up to the pier, no heavier than a sack of potatoes then bounded up after him.

"What's this about a famous singer?" Warren's eyes narrowed on Meggie.

Harry stepped in front of her, cutting off the man's sharp scrutiny. Another fellow moved into sight from the shadows. His fedora sat way back on hair slicked away from his forehead, beady eyes taking in every detail. Shit. Theodore Clifford. No need for the usual twist the man gave his stories that bordered on outrageous lies. In this case, Lady Margaret managed to hand him the story of the century.

"Warren," Harry snapped. "That ride?"

"Right. Sure. Marvin will get you to Mount Sinai straight away."

Harry shot Meggie a look over his shoulder. Lips pressed tightly together, she pulled her cap down to her eyes and moved up behind him. *Good girl.* He put his arm about Lewis, whose breathing had turned harsh and labored. "Let's go."

As they moved down the pier, Warren called out. "Harry, a man's been shot."

"Yeah, well he pulled a gun on the wrong man. The bastard's lucky he's not dead."

LADY MARGARET? LADY MARGARET Montley?"

Newshawk. Meggie recognized him from the club. Always standing about, small eyes set too close together, darting from socialite to shyster to any goose he might find news worthy. More times than she could count did Bernie and Eddie have something nasty to say when Mr. Clifford drummed up a non-existent row between the combo orchestra's—in her opinion—skirmishes that amounted to nothing more than slight artistic differences.

Take for instance, their appearance at WHN. Eddie was adamant the band stay true to their calling, singing before live audiences, where Bernie argued the more people who heard them the more likely the crowd would grow. Meggie tended to agree with Bernie, and had a sneaking suspicion that just Eddie feared new, unproven avenues or worse, failure. The whole idea was silly given how successful they'd become.

Not to mention Jess's reaction to every article that appeared in the Gazette. Her sniff of disgust when Mr. Clifford's latest fabricated piece showed up regarding the Bolshevik's. Meggie's stomach dropped and she tugged her cap down further almost covering her eyes. The man could destroy her career with the stroke of a pen.

Tendrils of panic started in the tips of her fingers and toes converged in her chest, squeezing the air from her lungs. Her gaze flicked over a greasy lock that had slipped loose. She quickly dropped her eyes.

"What a pickle you must find yourself in, hmm?"

She forced a low grunt passed her clogged throat and started around him.

"Back off, Teddy. This here's Sid. And he don't talk much." Harry's hand flattened against Mr. Clifford's chest and he pushed. Not so hard as to knock him to the ground. But Meggie knew Harry held himself back with tremendous effort.

"Say, what is this?" someone yelled.

She spun, momentarily caught by the excitement from behind. A large boat—well, not as big as the *Empress of India*, mind—eased into her view. Then upon closer scrutiny, a smaller vessel making its way in quickly.

"Hold up there, Harry."

"Christ," Harry muttered. He turned back toward the water. "What now, Warren? I gotta get my brother to the hospital."

"Looks like the Lighthouse Service might have a question or two for you."

"Marvin, get Lewis and Sid to the car. I'll only be a minute."

Once the smaller boat eased in to anchor, Harry pushed Meggie, none too gently, on the shoulder in Marvin and Lewis's direction. Meggie didn't hesitate. She ducked her chin and darted past the sleazy bloke and hurried after Lewis and their new chauffeur.

Just as Harry promised, he wasn't long. Fifteen minutes later they were on the bumpy road back to the city.

Harry scooted onto the backseat next to Lewis, and barked, "Let's go, Marvin" before he'd even shut the door. Marvin hit the gas, throwing up dirt and rocks in their wake.

"What'd they want, Harry?"

Meggie longed to hush Lewis. His raspy voice, a painful reminder of his ordeal. But she was glad he'd asked too, as she certainly couldn't.

"They had Legs and wanted the details. I gave them the short version," he said.

I want the details. Meggie wanted to shout.

Lewis gave a short laugh. After a moment he slumped against Harry and fell silent.

From the corner of her eye, Harry's clenched jaw looked as if it would break if the car hit a hard rut. But now that they were on their way back to the city and away from that newshawk, Meggie could feel the tension lifting from her as quickly as the rising sun.

The sky, though still a deep dark blue, was brushed with the softest pink, edging over the horizon. It offered the promise of an unusually crisp and bright November day. Nothing remotely similar to England's standards.

She reached across Lewis for Harry's hand then remembered the driver and pulled back. Her eyes flashed to the mirror where Marvin's were pinned on her.

Cheeks heated, she inhaled deeply and relaxed against the seat, cutting her gaze to Harry. She wasn't certain, but she could swear his lips twitched. The effect lessened the tightness about his mouth.

She released her breath with a vow. After this harebrained scheme, all future adventures were to receive a thorough plan of attack. The thought hit her hard in her chest. With all the danger she'd place herself in, *Harry in,* she'd still managed to not come up with the blunt Eliza needed to be free of indentured slavery. Her head fell back, and she closed her eyes, defeated. It was barbaric.

A warm hand covered hers and squeezed. Tears filled her eyes and she refused to look at him. Most especially when all she desired was to throw herself in the man's arms the way she had two nights ago. There she'd felt the promise of a different sort of adventure, a promise of warmth, and protection. Nothing remotely close to that fool Percy. A cold Englishman her mother seemed determined to force on her for life.

God, she was exhausted. Meggie willed the past few hours from her mind and took in deep, steady breaths. She reveled in Harry's presence despite the barrier his brother provided sitting between them.

LADY MARGARET MONTLEY'S FINGERS went slack against Harry's and he glanced over. Her forehead rested against the window pane, her chest rising then falling in a slow rhythm. He marveled at her ability to live in the moment. God, how he wished he shared such a gift, because sleep was a gift. One he'd embrace in *his* life.

Marvin must have realized the same. "Sid is an attractive fellow," he piped up. "All those soft curls and full lips are enough to turn a man."

"That's enough, Marvin." Harry's voice had lowered to a growl that bellowed deep.

"You seem awful possessive of this Sid." He chuckled. "Out cold, is she?"

Harry shook his head, refusing to answer. Harry couldn't deny it. Meggie was his—for the moment, anyway.

"What'd those lighthouse boys have to say?"

He met Marvin's eyes in the mirror. All mischief pushed aside, voice serious.

"Just what I said to Lewis. Legs was shot. Not dead, the lucky bastard. Guess they'll haul him to jail?"

"Hope they can make something stick this time. He's as slippery as they come."

"Kidnapping," Harry said with a bite. It was all he had. The problem, as he saw it, was that the hand who'd actually pulled the trigger, murdering Pa, belonged to Shaky-Alphonse. He glanced at Lewis. The morning sun, though still low in the eastern sky, showed his ashen pallor. When was the last time he'd had a decent meal?

God, had it been six weeks already since Pa had sent him on that fool's errand to check on Ma? Right at, he thought. On a day just like this one was shaping up to. No clouds marring a brilliant fall morning, unseasonably warm.

"I need you to run out to Queens, Harry." Pa hefted an outboard motor on his shoulder that had to weigh fifty pounds.

"Pa, let me handle the heavy lifting around here." Irritated, Harry took the motor from him. "Better yet, let Joe take it. What the hell do we pay him for?"

"Put it over there and get out to Queens. I have a meeting."

Harry hauled the motor to the table Pa indicated and set it down. "What kind of meeting? I can handle this shit, old man. You need to start looking at retirement." It was a strange request. Ma was probably soused already, besides.

"Damn it, not this again, Harry—"

"Hey, there, Pa. Harry."

Harry glanced over. Lewis was leaning on Roscoe, their head mechanic. "Shit, Pa. Lewis is drunk. We gotta do something about him. He's gonna hurt himself or someone else before all is said and done."

"Just get out to Queens," Pa snapped. "I'll take care of your brother. Now." Pa stormed off in Lewis's direction, jerked him by the arm and dragged him to the small office, slamming the door behind them.

What the hell? Harry forced himself to let it go, promising to address the matter with Pa again later. That night, at home.

But Pa and Lewis never made it home. Shaky-Alphonse, and most likely Legs Diamond, had paid Pa a visit, demanding Protection money. But Pa was a stubborn old man and refused to buckle. And, Harry learned, he was as proving just stubborn as his pa.

The car jerked to a stop, jolting Harry from the past, knocking Meggie's head against the window. "Ow."

He winced at the definitely feminine outburst and shifted his gaze to Marvin's. The twinkle of mischief was back. Harry shoved the door open and climbed out, sweeping Lewis up in his arms.

"I can walk, Harry. Put me down."

"You're more likely to faint like a girl," he retorted, carefully setting him to his feet.

Meggie slid along the seat and exited next, eyes narrowed on them. Harry held out a hand to assist her. Her gaze widened slightly and she shot the driver a glance over her shoulder.

"Marvin's great deductive skills saw past your "soft curls and full lips," Meggie." Harry smirked. "He's sharp, that Marvin." She sniffed her disdain at his outstretched hand. He ignored her rebuff and snatched her by the wrist, pulling her up and out of the car and into him. Her eyes flashed in surprise. A deep chuckled erupted from Harry. "Thanks for the ride, Marvin."

Marvin flashed a short wave, gunned the motor and took off.

MEGGIE STUMBLED BACK FROM Harry's hold, trying desperately to right her senses. She focused on a five-story building before her, constructed of brick and limestone. An elaborate carved cornice decorated the upper edge. The wrought iron fence surrounding the property added charm but looked to serve a second purpose with spiked tips on each post, spaced merely inches apart. Each level had its own balcony, the top one lined with bushes of greenery, though somewhat brown and thin, considering the time of year.

With his arm about Lewis, Harry strode to the portico. Meggie followed quickly, realizing the hospital was not too far from home. She reached Harry and Lewis as they stepped between two large columns that supported the protruding, flattened roof.

Once inside, Meggie found the noise deafening. She'd never actually visited a hospital before and the amount of people in this one was staggering. The entire scenario seemed a chaotic mess. Nurses darted about, some ushering patients; others attempting to calm screaming children; another rushed by carrying a stack of linen; yet another wielding a broom and dust bin. Meggie shuddered.

Harry snapped his fingers and, irritatingly, two— make that three nurses, who, of course, couldn't possibly be of the aged, homely variety—rushed over. A lovely brunette, sizing up the situation, snagged a wheeled chair and headed in their direction.

Meggie stood back, half tempted to rush back out the door. As if Harry read her mind, his hand snaked out and gripped her upper arm. Beautiful woman No. 1's eyes went wide as they roved over Meggie's unusual attire before stepping up to assist Lewis into the chair. After attempting to mask their giggles, No.'s 2 and 3 drifted off to assist others.

"Hello, doll," Lewis rumbled, and Meggie bit back a smile. "I'm yours for the takin'."

She turned a brilliant smile on him that moved swiftly to Harry, surprising Meggie with an urge to scratch her eyes out.

"The doctor will get with you as soon as possible, Mr. Dempsey." She spoke directly to Harry, forcing Meggie to swallow a groan. "Possibly an hour or so. As you can see—" Palm out, she indicated the ensuing disorder. "—we are a bit understaffed. If you follow this hallway to the fourth door on the left, there is a waiting area that should be a bit quieter."

"Thank you. That is much appreciated."

The nurse wheeled Lewis in the opposite direction. "Don't desert me, Harry," Lewis called out.

"Never again," Harry said. But the words were spoken softly and sounded like a promise to himself. Once Lewis disappeared from sight, Harry, still holding her arm, guided them to the waiting room the nurse had mentioned.

Meggie tried pulling her arm free to no avail. His grip tightened. Honestly, the man had no say over her nor any right to still be angry. They'd made it back unscathed, hadn't they? He probably wanted some simpering miss who jumped at the snap of his fingers, doted on his every word. Not a headstrong English Lady who took it into her head to dress as a boy—

"We're going to talk, Lady Margaret."

"Fine," she bit out. "But there is no need to manhandle me. I am not some unruly dog to be taken to heel."

"Someone needs to take you to heel." He reached the door and opened it.

It was somewhat quieter but there were hordes of people sitting and standing about. Harry let out an expletive and shut the door. His hand slipped down to hers and he pulled her after him, checking other doors along the corridor until he located a supply closet devoid of anyone. It was a good sized room, stuffed with shelves stocked with bandages, linens, cleaning supplies and other items Meggie couldn't begin to identify.

The minute Harry shut the rest of humanity away she jerked her hand from his and moved into an area out of direct site of the door. A nearby window with opaque glass let in light. Not that it distanced Harry, he just stalked her into a small open area that served as a place to hang things; a cubby of sorts.

"What the hell where you thinking? Dressing like a boy? Attempting to run with a bunch of thugs?"

Exhaustion, fear, frustration, and finally anger caught up and overwhelmed Meggie in the beat of a second. "I don't know." She swallowed back the tears. "I-I'm worried for my friend. She started a new occupation. I think she's in way over her head. She needs money to buy her way out of her contract."

"Contract! So, instead, you came up with some brilliant plan of your own. One that puts you in harm's way? Where's the logic in that?" Harry pushed a hand through his hair.

"I just wanted to help her."

"Damn it, Meggie. You need a keeper."

Fury roared through her, usurping her exhaustion. "I need no such thing, you-you *beast*. I had enough of that from my brothers." She lifted her chin. "Which is exactly the reason I sailed to America. To get out from underneath the domineering thumb of my overbearing family. Not to mention my mother's unrelenting matchmaking machinations."

"Dear God. Are you telling me that you took off for another country *on your own*?"

"Don't be ridiculous." She gave him her haughtiest look down her nose. "I came with three of my friends."

"And I'll wager not one of the four of you bothered sharing your plans with anyone."

"I'm a woman grown. I don't *need* anyone's permission to live my life, thank you very much."

Harry took her hand and tugged the snug glove from her hand one finger at a time.

Nice and slow, sending a thrill racing up her spine and other unmentionable places.

His pitch dropped, reverberated through her like a tightly stringed instrument. "Not even to keep you from gangsters like Legs Diamond or Shaky-Alphonse?"

He pocketed the one glove, then started on the other. "Who is Shaky-Alphonse?" The words came out in a tremble, husky and warm.

He grabbed her, pulled her into his hard body. "A dangerous man like me."

"You? You aren't dangerous, Harry." Her voice came out a whisper despite her attempts to appear unaffected.

He leaned in, his breath touching her lips. "Ah, but I'm very dangerous, Lady Margaret." His lips slid over hers, stealing her breath. He took her bottom lip between his teeth and bit down gently. Startled, her lips parted and his tongue scraped and danced over hers. It lasted but a second before he pulled back. Her fingers gripped the lapels of his coat.

"Yes," she said. "I-I see what you m-mean."

Eight

GOD. SHE TASTED AS sweet as his dreams promised. "I want you Meggie Montley. I want you so badly, I ache." He tugged her closer, her eyes widening. No doubt, at his erection pressed against her abdomen. He took her mouth again, pleased at her enthusiastic response. Harry fumbled with the buttons on her shirt, then reached for those luscious breasts. "What the hell?" He drew back frowning.

"What?" Her husky, breathless, yet puzzled voice threatened to send him over the edge. She glanced down then back up with a cheeky grin. "Oh. That."

He smoothed a palm over a wide strip of fabric that wrapped her chest that began just under her arms and spanned her ribs. "Yes, that," he growled.

"Well, I couldn't very well pass as a male with...with..."

He passed a hand over her flat stomach. "No, I don't suppose you could. Men certainly don't have such—" He turned a wolfish grin on her that set a deep blush in her cheeks. He dropped to his knees. "—enticing curves."

"W-what are you doing?"

He laid his lips on the silky skin of her stomach, dipped his tongue in the shallowed indentation of her navel. Her fingers latched into his hair, holding his head in, what he considered, the perfect position. "Have you ever made love, Lady Margaret?"

"In a supply closet?" Her voice hitched high.

His fingers gripped her waist, extending over slim hips. "Anywhere," he murmured against her stomach.

"N-no."

Harry fluttered light kisses over her exposed belly. With one hand he reached for the top fastener on her trousers.

The door flew back and two chattering voices entered. He froze. The grip on one side of his head loosened while the other tightened, entangled in his hair.

"The bulls are everywhere. Who do you suppose he is?"

"Grab some of those linens, would you? I heard Dr. Welks tell Nurse Thompson it was Jack Diamond. You know, Gentleman Jack. *Legs Diamond*. They worked him over in private."

A sharp gasp sounded from one of the intruders and Harry's fingers tightened on Meggie's hips. He glanced up and saw Meggie's hand covering her mouth, eyes squeezed shut. He forced his fingers loose. Her eyes opened and met his. Hell, he'd probably left a mark.

With luck, their two intruders would leave as quickly as they'd appeared.

"Lord, have mercy. The man is not so difficult to look at, is he?"

"Heaven's, Agnes, the man is a menace to society. He *kills* people." That shrill, nasal tone announced to the world how precarious Harry's own situation was.

As if he needed that reminder.

"Look at it this way, Eleanor. The man keeps us employed." She giggled and Harry wanted to throttle her.

"You are twisted, Agnes. Twisted." Their voices faded, the door latching with their exit.

Harry let out a breath, then rose to his feet. Desire slipped away, replaced with fear and, finally—common sense. Taking Meggie's shoulders, he shook her lightly.

"Damn it, you could have been killed. Legs Diamond isn't even dead."

"Who *is* this Diamond person? And why should he want to kill *me*?"

"Because he wants *me*." The urge to shout was overwhelming but he bit it back. "He murdered my father and kidnapped my brother. I'll wager I'm at the top of his hit list." The words spilled from him like volcanic ash.

Meggie's face paled as his words struck home. She shook her head. The tears filling her eyes tumbled over. "No. No. Nothing can happen to you, Harry."

He felt slightly nauseous in terrifying her so. But such rash behavior could only lead her into deeper trouble. How else was he to get through to her? Taking her head with both hands, he brushed her tears away with his thumbs.

"Nothing will happen to me." He kissed her gently. "But how am I supposed to keep you safe?"

Meggie's large blue eyes flashed in something like fury. Her hands flattened against his chest, and in one swift move, shoved. Shoved him hard, catching him off guard. The whole ridiculous scenario happened so fast, he found himself flat on his backside. Quickly rebuttoning her open shirt, she stuffed the shirt-tale in her trousers as if she were no stranger to wearing men's garb.

"What is it? What did I say?" Puzzled, he rose to sitting.

Meggie leaned down, outrage emanating like a fog. She poked a tapered nail in his chest. "No one appointed *you* bodyguard." She stepped over him, flung open the door and stormed out.

What the hell just happened? By the time Harry recovered his wits, two nurses reappeared, and started at his presence. He had no idea if they were the same women from before.

"Sir, this room is off limits to the public." At least one of them was, he decided. He didn't think he'd ever get that high-pitched shrill out of his head.

"Of course, ladies. My apologies." He darted around them and down the corridor. He reached the front doors in time to see Meggie's shapely buttocks disappearing down the street in a crush of people. Slowly, Harry turned back the way he'd come. Meggie was safe enough now in the light of day. He had other priorities. He needed to look after Lewis.

Tears streamed down Meggie's face. Blast that Harry Dempsey. She shoved them away only to be deluged with recurring rivulets that refused to dry up. Who did he think he was? Another one of her bossy siblings who'd never see her as an adult? Or worse, someone like her mother, set to see her married to some pasty-faced noble with no inclinations other than sitting about drinking day-in, day-out with his school chums. Or gadding about the globe, playing grown up with no meaning or yearning for life other than the next horse race? She'd throw herself off the tallest building in New York before allowing that to happen.

Meggie marched to the corner of Lexington and 67th. The man treated her like a recalcitrant child. Not like a woman who would adore him, cherish him, set him afire as he did her. She slumped against a light post, gulping back an outburst of sorrow.

"Get out of the way, Jobbie."

She glanced up, wondering where her hat had disappeared. Her hair blew free in the cool November breeze.

"Can't you see anything, Ralph? That ain't no jobbie, despite her outlandish attire."

An elderly woman whose height was lessened by her hunched shoulders reached out and patted Meggie's hand. "What is it, dearie? Man trouble?" She cut a look to the old geezer beside her. His thin, gray hair poked out from beneath a cap similar to the one Meggie had started the night with. "I'll wager it is. Take it from me. They're more trouble than they're worth."

"Then what in Sam's hell is she wearing boys' clothes for?"

Meggie's attempt at a smile fell short, but truly she was grateful.

"You know, I hate admittin' Ralph's right about anything," the old woman said, stuffing a tissue in Meggie's hand. "But if'n the boy means that much to ya, ye might try wearing things a little more feminine like. Why, a pretty little thing like you—" Her faded blue eyes narrowed. "In fact, ya look a teeny bit like that canary—"

Meggie wiped her nose. "Canary?"

But the woman would not be blustered. She wanted her say, and Meggie admired her for it. "That new up-and-coming singer. I heard her on the telegraphy."

"It's a radio, Doris. Let's go. I want my lunch."

"And I saw her picture in the newspaper. She was mite prettier than you with her light hair and smiling face."

Meggie's spirit lifted a little. "She was?"

Doris patted her hand again. "Ye take my word for it, dearie. Just dress like a girl—" Her eyes fell to Meggie's chest. "And, well, for most men a pretty face will do the trick."

The urge to giggle tickled Meggie's throat, but she maintained a straight face. She straightened from the light post and lifted her chin, a stubborn resolve setting deep inside. Harry thought of her as a child who needed looking after? Undisciplined, misbehaving, headstrong? Ha, the bloke will never know what hit him. "Thank you, Doris. May I call you Doris?"

"O'course you can, dearie. Me? I don't stand on no ceremony."

"I'll take your comments under advisement." Meggie glanced over at the scowling Ralph. "You'd best get Ralph fed, Doris. He looks hungry enough to eat a bear."

Doris peered at her companion. "Ain't it the truth. Ye take care now." With a short wave, Doris turned to Ralph who growled at Doris, but he took her hand and placed it on his arm. The sight melted Meggie as she watched them walk way, her heart suddenly full. With a lighter step she walked the two blocks east to Madison Avenue and caught the Fifth Avenue Coach to The Gables. Harry could wait until she'd had sleep.

Meggie stumbled into the flat, her light mood gone. Exhausted, frustrated and failure weighed her down. What would she tell Eliza?

The smell of burnt scones assaulted her. Charli, shoulders shaking, stood bent at the tiny kitchen sink, hot pad in one hand clutching an empty baking sheet.

Meggie rushed and wrapped an arm about her friend, pushing a strand of her red hair from her tear stained face. "Charli, it's just a batch of scones. The next group will turn out fine. I'm certain of it."

Charli shook off her hold and stepped back. "No! It won't. Nothing will ever turn out right for me. Ever," she shouted. "You. You don't know anything, Lady *Perfect*." The baking sheet clattered in the sink. She turned and dashed to her and Eliza's curtained off bedroom.

Meggie stood there, stunned. Even at Meggie's and Jess's constant razzing at Mrs. Greensley's Charli had never reacted so...so vehemently. And Lord knows, she and Jess had certainly deserved Charli's wrath, or worse, on more than one occasion.

Tears pricked Meggie's eyes. *Lady Perfect indeed*. God, if only. Meggie made her way to her room and jerked the curtain closed. She wished she could curtain off her thoughts as easily. Collapsing down on her perfectly made bed, she listened for sounds from Charli's and Eliza's room.

She caught a sniffle from Charli, but nothing else. No chatter from Eliza, and Jess was clearly working late.

Charli would not welcome her intrusion, and fatigue robbed Meggie of further coherence. She tugged the coverlet up from the side of the bed without rising and closed her eyes. She would rest, just for a moment, then talk to Charli...*just for a moment*.

HARRY HAD NO CHOICE. Meggie Montley was out of his league. Not only was she scads above him in class, but her career was set to take off for the stars, and he refused to be the one responsible for standing in her way. The woman lived and breathed a sensuality that knocked him senseless. Just look how Ma had resented Pa. Harry would rather cut off his arm than have Meggie sneer such resentment in his direction.

"Mr. Dempsey?"

Harry glanced up at the petite nurse who had wheeled Lewis down the corridor earlier.

"The doctor will see you now, Mr. Dempsey."

Harry pulled himself to his feet and followed her past a desk where several volunteers sat behind. Past a large room lined with beds protruding out from the walls along both sides, each separated with a chair. There must have been forty beds in that one room, and not a single empty. They passed another three rooms, each the same. Only the faces were different. At the end of the long hall she turned into another room, this one devoid of the number of people. Antiseptic hit him full force.

"Where is Jack Diamond?"

The pretty little brunette kept walking but threw over her shoulder, "He was released."

"I'd heard he'd been shot." Harry almost laughed, but it wasn't funny.

"Just grazed, sir. He was treated, then released with a police escort."

He grunted, somewhat relieved at that bit of information. But, hell, some of the coppers were more crooked than the criminals.

"Here we are," she chirped. "Mr. Dempsey?"

"I told you, doll. I'm Lewis. Mr. Dempsey is the flat tire standing behind you." Lewis laughed a grousing sound that despite his words, made Harry feel better.

"And I told you, *Mr.* Dempsey, the name is Nurse Gladys, not doll." She snapped the covers up to Lewis's neck but tucked them around him more gently than he deserved.

"Mr. Dempsey? I'm Dr. Jolston. Your brother here, I'm surprised to say, will live. He hasn't taken much care with his body, I daresay." His clipped British accent reminded him of Meggie's. "He's malnourished and bruised. But insists upon leaving. Can't say as I recommend it, but being short on beds, I'm willing to place him in your care."

"Thank you, Doctor. I'll see that he is well-provided for."

The doctor scribbled something on a board he held, then ripped the page away and handed it to Harry. "There you are then. Just show this to the women at the desk on your way out." He gave a short nod and disappeared as quickly as he'd appeared.

Damn, croakers. Harry didn't trust the lot of them. "Come on, brother. Let's blow this popsicle stand. It's time to send a little happiness Ma's way."

W<small>HERE'S</small> M<small>EGGIE</small>!"

Truly? Jessie's screech could wake the dead. Meggie squinted into the waning light from a crease in the curtain, head pounding. Maybe she was dead. Her mouth was dry like she'd imbibed too much gin. The single overhead light bulb flickered to life and Meggie blinked against the intrusion.

Jessie was still dressed in her office attire that consisted of a plaid pencil skirt, topped with a hip length mulberry cardigan. "Is this true?" She rattled the paper she held in one hand.

"Is what true?" Meggie's voice croaked with sleep as she pulled herself to sitting.

Her eyes flicked over Meggie. "Oh my God. It is." She sank down on the bed beside her. "You're wearing boys' clothes. You've made the papers—again!" She snapped the paper out and read:

"*Lady Margaret turned Lady Bootlegger? Or Lady Copper?*

New York City is in for a surprise. The sultry canary, English Miss, Lady Margaret Montley was spotted early this morning dressed in boy's garb accompanied by none other than Harry Dempsey. You may remember Mr. Dempsey's father who was allegedly murdered by Shaky-Alphonse in recent weeks, believed in some circles that Gentleman Jack "Legs" Diamond as the culprit behind the hit when the elder Dempsey refused to pay out protection money for his Marina Supply Company.

Seen with Harry was his thought-dead brother, Lewis Dempsey. Sources refused to confirm that Legs was shot sometime in the early morning hours. But he was taken into custody by the police from the US Lighthouse Service. Rumor has it that Mr. Diamond was treated and released from Mount Sinai Hospital in police custody as this story went to press.

Several questions beg asking: who shot Legs Diamond this time? Has Lady Margaret turned Lady Bootlegger? Was Harry Dempsey out for revenge?

Your faithful news reporter — Theodore Clifford"

Jessie lowered the paper. "Is it true, Meggie?"

Meggie flopped back on the bed and covered her eyes with the crook of her bent arm. "I never saw this Legs Diamond."

"It is true." Jessie whispered. "You reckless girl. You could have been killed. What on earth drove you to do such a thing?"

Meggie sat up again. Charli and Eliza appeared in the doorway, and Meggie smiled wryly at Charli. "I guess I'm not so perfect after all, am I?"

"I should have never said that, Megs. I'm so sorry." Her mouth turned down, regretful.

Jessie rolled the paper and smacked Meggie on the arm. "Don't ever do something like that again. At least not without me."

"I'm sorry. I didn't mean to worry anyone."

Jess hugged her. "We know you didn't, darling. Now, I have a date tonight." Eliza stepped in the room, allowing Jessie to leave with Charli.

Alone with Eliza, seeing her pasty face, tears clogged Meggie's throat. "I'm so sorry, Eliza. I wanted to get you the money, but I completely failed you."

"No. No, don't ever say that." Eliza hugged Meggie. "I can't believe you did that—*for me*."

"Don't you see? It was all for nothing." Meggie raised her gaze. Pools of moisture shimmered in Eliza's eyes.

"No. Please, Meggie," she whispered. Eliza straightened then squared her shoulders. "I have wonderful news. The contract's been paid. Mr. Taggart paid it. He paid the entire thing off. I'm free and clear."

Meggie narrowed her eyes on her. "That sounds quite marvelous. Almost unbelievably so."

Eliza returned Maggie's stare, blinking only once. "Yes, quite. I was surprised myself, but he's English. He was delighted to come across a Brit with housekeeping experience." A soft smile touched her lips. "You may meet him if you wish."

That was a surprise. Meggie studied her friend's wide-hazel eyes carefully. After a long moment, she let out a long stream of air, convinced Eliza was telling the truth. She pulled her in another hug. A second later she felt Eliza's relief escape in a shuddered breath.

"Thank God, Eliza. Thank God."

Nine

Meggie worked her way past the slew of cheers, well-wishers and exclamations of shock of having survived her ordeal from the previous night. Her step was lighter. Eliza was okay, and that was the most important thing. Meggie eked her way through the crowd, bound for the stage. Bernie's shiny, bald head was lowered and his fingers tapped the cymbals lightly. He glanced up and a smirk tilted his lips. "Well, if it ain't our own Baby Vamp."

The other boys chuckled but continued with their warm up. She scowled at them. "I hate to even ask what that means."

"Ain't nothin' but a popular female, doll. What the hell were you thinkin'? Did you shoot Gentleman Jack?" The others stopped what they were doing and peered at her, interest obvious.

"I never saw Gentleman Jack. Blast, there's no proof it was even me! You didn't see my picture in the paper, did you?"

"Lady Margaret?"

Meggie spun and found herself standing a few inches over a portly fellow with a double-chin and thick, black mustache. A receding hairline made him appear older, but his youthful face attested him somewhere in his early to mid-thirties.

He took her outstretched hand. "Allow me to introduce myself. I'm Paul Whiteman." At her gasp of surprise, he went on. "And, this here—" He indicated another man beside him, tall, slender and attractive with light brown, wavy hair. "—is George Gershwin."

Mr. Gershwin gave a short incline of his head. "A pleasure," he murmured.

"You've created quite the stir, Lady Margaret." Mr. Whiteman laughed, sending a blush of heat that spread from her neck up.

She'd donned the silver-sequined number she'd worn for the masquerade aboard the *Empress of India,* and was certain her skin, red and mottled, clashed horribly. "It's a pleasure to meet you, Mr. Whiteman. I-I don't know what to say." Surely, he would forgive her unrefined stammering. He was renowned and he *knew her by name.* Meggie felt a little faint at the notion.

He led her to a nearby table, shooing away patrons already seated, and guided her into a vacated chair. "I like your moxy. I have a proposition for you."

Indignation curdled her stomach and she started to rise.

Mr. Whiteman's hands came up, palms out in a defensive motion. "Calm yourself, Lady Margaret. George here will be playing with my orchestra at the Plaza on election-Tuesday. One of the largest Voting Parties in the country, and we'd like you to sing."

Stunned and speechless, Meggie could only stare at the two men.

"You are already a sensation, Lady Margaret, but quite frankly, I can catapult you to the moon and back. So, what do you say? The Plaza on Tuesday?"

Unable to utter a single word, Meggie just nodded.

"Excellent. That is just excellent, Lady Margaret." Mr. Whiteman took her hand and pressed his lips to her knuckles. "Until Tuesday then."

By the time Meggie croaked out a "thank you" they were gone.

"Megs?"

She blinked and Charli was standing before her.

"Megs, you're going to have to move." Charli looked over her shoulder. "Ira is getting angry. This table is for paying customers."

"Oh, of course, Charli. Sorry." Meggie stood quickly but her path was suddenly blocked by another gentleman of a stocky and broad, muscular build. His nose was crooked like he'd spent a lifetime fighting. His newsboy cap was pulled low over his face.

"You a friend of Eliza Gilbert's?"

"Yes." She spoke slowly, the fine hairs at her nape rising. His aggressive stance had her taking a step back. She glanced around but Charli was already at the bar refilling her tray with drinks. "What do you want with Eliza?"

"I want information."

Her chin went up. She gave him her Mrs. Greensley's coldest stare. "Today is not your lucky day, sir. I don't give out information on my friends."

"P'haps I should start again, ma'am."

"Perhaps you should."

"I'm trying to find out something about a missing girl."

Meggie swallowed. "N-not the ...dead girl found in the alley?"

His lips pursed. "No. Not Roxy Gould. I'm looking for Cynthia Yost, my ex-fiancée," he said harshly. "Your friend, Eliza, knows something but she won't come clean, bein' quite the skilled fabricator she is."

Meggie's hand landed in a solid crack across the bounder's face. His cap flew to the ground, revealing a shock of dark blond hair that was a tad too long. The instruments behind her screeched to silent. He shocked her with a smile, showcasing a dimple that creased the right side of his face.

HARRY TOSSED BACK HIS WHISKEY welcoming the burn down the back of his throat. He signaled for another, pissed that a blonde, sultry bearcat had the ability to knock off his carefully managed existence. Her silver gown did nothing to stem his careening desire. The low-cut bodice that shaped her bust so perfectly had him wishing she still wore the bindings and buttoned up shirt and bowtie from two nights ago. Those assets should be for his eyes only. He groaned. And this was exactly the reason he should stay away from her.

She should have already been crooning *It Had To Be You.* But no. Some short, fat man had led her to a table, talking ninety to nothing. Harry couldn't make out the egg's words, but when Meggie's lips tightened and hands fisted, Harry rose.

A second later, the gent's hands lifted, palms face-out, and her expression softened into something rhapsodic. The second whiskey appeared on the table. Harry lowered back down and snatched it up. And he damn sure didn't like the looks of the younger man who nodded to her. *Meggie was his.* He swallowed another hit. *But she wasn't, was she.* He'd already made it clear he couldn't keep her safe.

His lip curled. As if she'd cared.

Meggie's eyes grew wide at something the round man said, then she nodded. A minute later the two men were making their way through the crowd. Harry's eyes followed them to the door but not before Markov hurried over to them in all his elegance, shaking their hands. By the time Harry's gaze settled on Meggie again, another man dressed no better than a dock worker had her cornered. Enough was enough. He threw back the rest of the whiskey and stormed his way over.

He made an effort to stuff the envy. Seeing the two in a standoff, sparks flying, was somewhat reassuring. He reached Meggie's side just as her hand landed upside the gent's face to stun the surrounding crowd into silence.

Rather than anger, the man smiled at Meggie, sending Harry's blood surging.

He swooped his cap from the floor and tipped his head. "I do hope Miss Gilbert appreciates such loyalty." He spun on his heel and disappeared through the gathering mass of onlookers.

"Miss Gilbert?" Harry took Meggie's trembling hand and followed her gaze after the hulk. "If I'm not mistaken, that's Vincent Taggart."

"I don't care who he is. He had no call to insult my friend." Meggie bit her bottom lip, and damned if Harry wasn't tempted to drag her back through the secret hallway and have his way with her. "Who is Vincent Taggart?"

"Vincent "The Fist" Taggart. Only the best prize fighter, next to Dempsey—a…er…cousin of mine…" Harry cleared his throat.

She tossed her unfashionable curls, the fire back in her eyes. "Still—"

Harry cut her off and snagged her arm. "Come on. I have something for you." He led her to the bar, then touched the panel to the side, dragging her through the secret door.

"What are you up to, Harry? I have to sing in another fifteen minutes."

"This won't take long," he growled. At the first open room, he pulled her inside. And because he couldn't resist, slid his mouth over hers. He savored the sweet taste of mint before his tongue demanded the same. His palms curled Meggie's slender neck. Her pulse beat against his thumb, his erection pressed against her. If he didn't stop, he'd find himself unable to at all. He pulled away.

"Harry?" Her whisper slid over his skin like the finest silk. That pulse against his thumb, fast and erratic.

"I have something for you, Meggie." He pulled the folded envelope from the inside pocket of his coat.

She took it with shaking fingers. "What is this?"

He watched her expression, waiting for the moment she threw herself in his arms. It was everything he had in the world.

"Cash?" Shock colored the one word in something like a hiss.

Not quite the reaction he was expecting. "What is it? What's wrong?"

She slammed the money in his chest along with the realization that he couldn't put her from his life. He needed Lady Margaret Montley as a permanent fixture in his life.

"How dare you! I am *not* for sale, Mr. Dempsey!" She tore from the room as if Legs Diamond suddenly appeared pointing a pair of Smith & Wessons on her.

"It's for your friend." But he was already speaking to an empty room. Damn it. That girl belonged on Broadway. Her exits were spectacular.

Ten

Three days later

MEGGIE, YOU HAVE GOT to stop crying. We only have three hours before you are expected at the Plaza to perform in front of all those people. Important people, Meggie. It's their big election day. Georgie is on his way over. He's bringing every arsenal in his bag of tricks."

Meggie sat at the rickety kitchen table with Jessie standing behind her, holding her favorite silver-handled brush. Jessie stuffed a dainty lace handkerchief in her hands, and Meggie pressed it to her eyes. The tears flowed like the river that's dam had burst.

"Those circles beneath your eyes are as deep and dark as the English Channel," Jessie went on. "That damn Harry Dempsey. I have half a mind to bop him on the head the next time I see him."

Her sobs slowed to hiccups and she peered in the table top mirror. Jess was right. She looked like the devil. "You and me both. But I'm sure I've seen the last of him…" The words trailed off into another onslaught.

"What I don't understand is why he had an envelope full of cabbage."

Meggie looked at her.

Jess shrugged. "That's what the boys at the *World* call blunt."

"That's the dumbest thing I've ever heard in my life," she muffled in her tissue.

"Tell me, Megs. Why would he attempt to pay you?"

The question infuriated her all over again. "Because, he thinks I can be bought like some cheap floozy—" Meggie's back stiffened.

Jess pulled the brush through her hair. "What?"

"He must have thought I still needed—" Meggie dropped her head in her hands. "I'm such a fool."

Meggie raised her head, meeting Jessie's narrowed eyes in the mirror. "Why would Harry think you needed that much money? Did you even count it?"

"No," she said softly. "But I'll wager it equaled a thousand quid."

Jess's hand flew to her chest and she stumbled into another chair. "Dear God, Meggie. A thousand dol—why, that's a fortune. Why? Why do you need that much money?"

Meggie squirmed under Jess's scrutiny. "It wasn't for me."

"Then who?" Jess fairly shouted.

"Eliza!" she burst out. Her hand flew over her mouth. At Jess's puzzled expression, Meggie drew in a deep breath. "Eliza got in a bit of a bind."

"What kind of bind, Megs?"

"It's okay now, Jess. Really, it is. Eliza told me yesterday everything is taken care of. I need to find Harry. Apologize to him. He was only trying to help." Meggie stood quickly as the tears gathered and fell once again. "I have to find him."

The door flew back. Georgie stood there blocking any exit, make-up satchel in hand. "Darling, *you* are going nowhere looking like the drowned rat you do. We have work to do. Now, sit!"

HARRY SHOVED HIS HANDS in the front pockets of the only black suit he owned and ignored the politicians, newshawks, society bigwigs—all a bunch of swells and high-hats in his book—while they meandered about shaking hands, and kissing asses. His gaze was locked on the orchestra members making their way to the elevated stage setup, instruments in hand. Not the six-piece combo of Bernie and Edison's little six-piece orchestra. No, this was the big-time. At last count there were seventeen pieces, not including the shiny black grand, currently being rolled out onto a pink marble floor. He snorted. *Pink.* The elaborate ballroom suited Lady Margaret, right down its ornate chandeliers embellished in gold, and the mirrored surfaces, decorating the walls. Harry felt as if he'd stepped into a French Chateau straight out of the early 1800s. Close to a hundred white, small, round tables were placed strategically back from an area reserved for dancing. Each adorned with a single, long-stemmed rose—*red*—in a crystal vase.

The sight of those roses filled his head with images running amok. Meggie throwing her body into his, sliding down his own hard body; his hands clasping hers as he tugged her into the darkened hallway at Club 501. Dropping to his knees, where his lips found the silky, bare skin of her belly. Every thought screaming what could have been. What should have been.

Knots cramped his stomach. He hadn't seen her since Saturday night, when she'd mistaken his intentions of handing over every last dime of his savings. He'd been so angry he'd stormed out of Club 501 and high-tailed it home, deciding to check on Ma and Lewis. Regret had him rushing back. But by that time, the band was tearing down and Meggie was long gone.

So here he stood, at Frank Markov's invitation, whom had also disappeared. Waiting, *hoping* for the opportunity to share just a few words with her. Explain how he'd only wanted to help her friend. Tell her—tell her that *he loved her.* If she blew him off after that, then he would let her go—*bullshit*. No. No way in hell was he prepared to walk away.

He scanned the ballroom as more patrons crowded their way in from an opulent foyer, frowning when Teddy Clifford ambled in flashing his press pass as if it were the key to the city. The man was still a sleaze, no matter how decked out he was.

As the band members tuned up, Paul Whiteman's thick mustache seemed to twitch, his movements agitated. The whole scenario set the hair at Harry's neck rising. There was no sign of Meggie. Nothing strange about that, but Harry ventured closer. He couldn't quell the sensations. Sensations that rang all too familiar when Pa sent him on a fool's errand just before he was brutally murdered.

The need to see Meggie surged through him. His skin pricked with apprehension and he hastened his steps. A scrawny fellow brushed by reaching Whiteman just before Harry.

"What the hell do you mean she left?"

"I'm sorry Mr. Whiteman. I-I was checking on her as you asked but she was halfway down the hall with some palooka. Looked like he been done over but good. Face was all banged up."

"Son of a bitch," Harry hissed.

The two men's gazes jerked to his.

"You know anything about why my star canary would scram fifteen minutes before Showtime?" Whiteman demanded.

Harry sucked in a deep breath. "Keagan," he said.

THE DRESSING ROOM DOOR opened then clicked shut. Meggie glanced in the mirror to see who else had come to wish her well. First, Jess, then Charli had visited. No sign of Eliza *or* Harry. She froze. Alarm hit her veins. But it felt as if her movements were hindered; like swimming through molasses. She stood from the vanity table and turned. Long gone was Joey Keagan's neatly slicked back hair and dapper matching argyle socks and sweater he'd sported the last time she'd seen him. He still wore them, but now they were ripped and soiled beyond repair. The stench emanating from him reminded her of something vile dredged up from the Thames.

"I've nothing to say you, so you may as well leave." Damn her shaky voice.

He sneered. "You think you're better than me? I told you before—you and me, we could make thousands. Instead, you throw yourself into the arms of the closest lug. Fuck that Harry Dempsey. In fact, I'm guessing you already have."

Meggie's cheeks burned, not because she had been with Harry, but because she so wanted him in that very way.

Joey ran a hand over his bruised jaw. "Well, I'll take my due with or without your say so."

Fury poured through her. "Are you insane? I'm singing in fifteen minutes. I'm not going *anywhere* with you."

He blocked the door, standing with legs spread, arms folded over his chest. "You're nothing but a quiff, and I'll have my way with you yet."

Meggie's anger began to give way to fear. "You think I'm going to just walk out of here? With you?" She forced a laugh, suddenly realizing her mistake in hesitating. She'd given him too much time to ensconce himself. She should have lunged at him, gouged out his eyes, brought him to his knees with a pointed kick. Yes, Eliza *had* taught her that little maneuver. She tamped down her panic. She would just have to wait out the next opportunity to execute the move.

He straightened and slipped his hands into the pockets of his tattered tweed jacket and pulled out a small gun. "I happened to think that's exactly what you'll do." His gaze swept from her face to her feet and back, settling on her cleavage. "That blue sequined stuff looks mighty fine, but I expect you'll need a coat for our little adventure."

Someone pounded on the door. "Five minutes, Miss Montley."

She opened her mouth to call out, but the hammer on the pistol clicked and the words stuck in her throat.

He let out a low chuckle that would haunt her dreams for life. "We'll have to do something about your name. After a while we can set you up like one of those courtson's." He inclined the gun toward the coat tree in the corner. "Let's go."

Meggie snatched up the dark, blue and black tapestry weaved coat with fur cuffs and collar she'd found in a second hand store somewhere near 6th Avenue and 42nd Street and slipped it on. "Courtesan. If you are going to use the word, you should at least make an effort to pronounce it correctly," she snapped.

Joey stepped closer and fingered the collar, his wrist brushing her chin. "Nice."

She jerked back.

"We'll have none of that *Lady* Margaret," he said, gripping her arm. "By the time I'm done with you, you won't be a *lady* anything. Well, perhaps a lady of the night." He laughed at his silly joke, lifting her chin with the barrel. He pressed it into her skin.

Terror speared her spine, racing up then down.

"We'll just quietly make our way out. There's doors all over this place. But one wrong move and I'll knock you off and anyone who comes close. I may not live through it, but neither will you. You understand?"

She could barely nod. She buttoned her coat and put her chilled hand in her pocket. *The pocket that held her flat key*.

Still gripping her other arm, he jerked her to the door. He slipped the gun into his pocket and eased the door back. After checking the corridor, he tugged her out, strolling just as nice as you please.

"Miss Montley?" The words sounded behind.

Joey picked up their pace and snarled, "Not a word."

Another wave of anger surged through her. She refused to make it easy for him. "You'll never get away with this, you know. I'm not even wearing a hat. Women just do not go about without a hat."

"Shut your trap," he bit out.

But Meggie was afraid. She clutched the clunky metal between her fingers, praying for an opportunity, *any* opportunity, because just ahead on the left were doors facing the north, and across the street from that, Central Park. At this time of year, he could stash her anywhere. That was if he didn't kill her first. At least there were people around now—

"Hold it right there, Keagan."

The deep, menacing voice was so low Meggie stumbled over it, her fear reaching the clouds. All she could envision was the man she loved bloodied and sprawled at her feet. "Harry. He's got a gun." Her trembling voice squeaked. She gripped her inadequate, but only, weapon tighter.

"So do I. Move away from her, Keagan, before I blow your brains out all over her pretty dress."

"You fucked with my life enough, Harry. Now I'm gonna fuck with yours—"

Meggie didn't wait another second. She jammed the spiked heel of her t-strapped shoe into his foot. Her motion caught him by surprise enough to loosen the grip he had on her arm. She threw her elbow into his stomach, then spun. With a pained grunt Joey bent forward. Then with the key positioned between her index and middle fingers she went for the kill—but missed his eye, only managing to clip his neck strong enough to draw blood.

She was flung against the wall like a rag doll but somehow managed to stand by her own two legs. Joey slid to the floor out cold. Blood trickled from the side of his head co-mingled with the wound on his neck.

Chest heaving, her pulse raced, her cries whimpered. "Is he d-dead?" The words landed in the warmth of Harry's neck and she shuddered in his hold. Perhaps she should rethink this being famous business. Between the coppers who'd raided the 501, and some brow-beating bully accosting her at the Plaza—she shuddered.

"Not from lack of trying," Harry growled. "Nice work, Lady Margaret. You are quite resourceful." His breath teased the hair at her temple.

"I have three b-bothersome b-brothers." Things would be fine. She just needed to stay calm. *And here was Harry, coming through yet again.*

"Come on, you have the performance of a lifetime to give. And you're already late." His gentleness brought tears to her eyes. "And then? We need to talk."

Eleven

"OH. MY. GOD." TEARS pooled in Jessie's eyes, along with the words that had Meggie sniffing back her own. The problem, as Meggie saw it, was that once she let loose a river, then all was lost. Not one who cried prettily or, in most cases, often—just lately.

Jess was waiting in Meggie's dressing room when she'd arrived. "You were fabulous." She threw her hands in the air and spun about like a ballerina in a perfect turn. All those dance lessons Lady Hatton had forced on her paid off. She stopped and lifted her chin—another Lady Hatton inheritance. "But, then, I knew you would be."

Meggie grinned, because she just couldn't help it. "I was, wasn't I?" She faced herself in the mirror, snatched a tissue and dabbed at her tears, refusing to turn into another blubbering mess before her face-off with Harry. She needed every arsenal for the talk he was demanding. Her premonitions for these things was quite reliable and she would not let him brush her away. *Not again*.

"What did Whiteman say afterwards? I saw him tell you something. You looked positively vapor-struck when he walked away?"

Meggie's hands flew to her mouth and she spun back to her friend. "Oh, Jess. He's been asked to compose music for a new Broadway show and asked that I audition." With each word her voice went up an interval until it ended an octave higher and on a squeal.

The room filled with stunned silence, Meggie's eyes meeting Jess's. A second later Jess's screams met Meggie's, and Jessie pulled her into a hug. "You did it, Megs. You truly did it. You made it without any help with your interfering brothers and your mother's disapproving airs. You'll never have to marry that icky Percy. Or anyone if you don't so chose."

The words caught Meggie by surprise, reeling her back from the clouds she'd just been floating on. *Harry. I would marry Harry.*

Someone banged on the door, startling them. "Everything all right in there?"

Before she could answer the door crashed back. An attendant was righting himself then skittered off. Harry moved into the doorframe, then like a cat strolled inside. Serious and unsmiling, solid—steady, strong. Tempting Meggie to throw herself into arms that would always keep her grounded.

Jess squeezed her in another hug and slipped away, leaving Meggie on her own, to fight the battle of her life.

HARRY COULDN'T GET A read from the wide-blue, unblinking eyes peering at him. "Huh. So you never wish to marry? And who the hell is Percy?" The statements had thrown him. How the devil was he supposed to convince Meggie that he was the man for her? The *only* man for her.

She blinked.

Unnerved and off his game, Harry blundered in, pushing the door to until it latched. Meggie's eyes widened slightly. The only sign showing she was not as confident as she pretended. She dropped into the chair before the mirror and picked up a silver-handled hairbrush, fingers trembling. Another encouraging sight.

"I believe I mentioned that before."

"No. No, I would have remembered you saying that." He sauntered closer, relieved and itching to run his fingers through locks that were once again the blonde, soft curls he loved, the brown rinse completely washed away from her adventure several nights ago.

"Oh. For years I've been living under the pressure of being manacled to some pale-faced noble with no ambition. Something of which, I have no desire."

He took the brush from her hand, surprised at how heavy it was. "I see." He slid it through her hair, met her eyes in the mirror. "I'm glad you don't sport that short wavy do most of the young women are wearing these days."

"But I could," she said softly.

He set the brush aside and fingered the softness of her hair while he considered her response. "Yes, you could. But it wouldn't stop me from wanting you in my bed every night for the rest of my life."

Her eyes went wide again, then narrowed on him. "What exactly are you saying, Mr. Dempsey?"

As stern as she tried to appear her bottom trembled, touching something deep within his chest. He felt a smile play about his lips, desire spiraling through him. His hands moved to her shoulders and he swiveled her around. He lowered himself to his knees where they were face to face.

"I mean it, Harry. Despite—" She paused, took a steadying breath. "I can't be bought."

He opened his mouth to explain. Tell her that the money was just a misunderstanding, but she stayed him with an index finger to his lips. His own pulse tripled. He resisted, with great effort, of sucking her finger into his mouth, but couldn't keep his tongue from one irresistible lick.

Heat flooded her cheeks, coinciding with her sharp intake of air. Another thread bonded her to him. An unbreakable tie.

"I realized later that the money...the money was most likely for my friend."

He nodded.

"Still, my brothers would hunt you down and dig your heart out with a dull spoon if they caught wind of—"

"Stop. I've heard enough." His tone came out darker, harsher than he'd intended. "Do you really believe I'd want you without binding you to me forever?" He snorted, disgusted. "Leave you an easy way to escape?"

Her eyes softened and the lodge in his chest gave way.

"Hell, no. I want you with me. Always. Inevitably tied by matrimony."

Her eyes shimmered, and the sight filled him with hope.

"I'm not an easy man, Lady Margaret. But I'll never stand between you and your dreams."

One tear spilled over. Only one.

He wiped it away with his thumb. "I love you. I didn't need to be at Frank's every night. I was there because I couldn't stay away from *you*."

She launched from the chair and into his arms. "Don't ever scare me like that again." Her sobs soaked his collar and he tightened his arms around her. "Ever."

"No," he whispered. "Never."

~*~THE END~*~

Dear Reader,

We chose the 1920s because, at the time, the remake of The Great Gatsby was coming out later that year. In fact, we were so excited that we had a 20's theme party at our favorite gather place, The Martini Lounge in Edmond, Oklahoma.

Writing in a time period you have little knowledge regarding is fascinating. So much to learn. One of the things I learned was that the US Coast Guard had not yet formed. It was the US Lighthouse Service – a branch of the government that later became a part of the US Coast Guard.

I also learned how quickly technology was growing regarding the telephone systems, subway system in New York City and radio stations.

Incorporating of each of these things in my story was both, challenging and fun. I hope you enjoyed reading our series as much as we had fun writing them!

If you have any inclination, a review would be most welcome, as they important to authors. Yes, the bad ones as well.

Read ahead for introductions to Rebellious, Ruined and Runaway. And please accept my most sincere thanks.

Happy Reading ~~ Kathy L Wheeler

Rebellious

Amanda McCabe

Prologue

England, 1924

SUCH A LOVELY BRIDE! The Hattons have certainly made a big production of this wedding, haven't they?"

"Wouldn't *you*, if you were them? Now they have one less hoydenish daughter to be rid of."

Lady Jessica Hatton choked on her forbidden cigarette as a laugh almost burst out of her at the two fusty old dowagers' words. Lady Briggsly and Mrs. Cartwright, the two biggest gossips around. They made it sound as if her parents had a whole tribe of flappers running loose in the ancient corridors of Hatton Hall. That sounded as if it would be quite fun, but alas there was only herself and her older sister Lulu, the newly disposed-of bride. And Lulu had never been at all hoydenish.

Jess, on the other hand...

Jessica slid down lower in her hiding place in the hollow of the huge old oak tree. The grove of trees was far beyond the huge white pavilions set up for Lulu and David Carlisle's wedding reception. She'd thought no one would venture away from the caviar and pate, and all that free champagne. The sky was just turning pinkish at the edges as the sun sank lower, and the music was growing louder.

But nowhere was safe. Not at the Wedding Of The Year, according to *Town Talk* magazine.

Jessica took another drag on her cigarette, and prayed the guests would wander away soon.

"Well, Lady Louisa looked beautiful, I'll certainly give her that," one of the dowagers sniffed. "I heard they went to Paris to get the gown from Monsieur Poiret. As if Lucille of London wasn't grand enough."

"They had to distract everyone from the bridegroom, didn't they?" said her friend. "Poor man. He was so handsome once. I'm surprised Lady Louisa put back her veil to look at him."

Jessica nearly leaped out out of her hidey-hole at those nasty words. David Carlisle was a war hero, once the best friend of their lost brother Bill, and the sweetest chap that ever lived! His scars only proved his bravery. If those old cows would just...

But then she remembered her mother's stern admonition before they climbed into the car to go to the church. *No scenes today, Jessica, I am warning you! No pranks at all. This is your sister's day.*

So Jess had once let a frog loose at the cake table at a wedding. That was ages ago, when she was just a silly child, and it had been that snooty Millicent Haigh's reception anyway. She rather deserved the uproar.

But not Lulu and David. Their day had to be perfect, and it was. All clouds of tulle, orange blossoms, towering white cakes of spun sugar, and joyful smiles in two lives that had seen too much sadness. Jess would never do anything to mar that. Even now.

Yet she couldn't help but blow a ring of silvery smoke toward those old biddies.

"Do you smell something?" one of the ladies shrieked. "Charlotte, you would never do such a thing as smoke would you?"

Jessica peeked out again to see that Lady Briggsly was holding her poor daughter, Charlotte Leighton, who had once been Jess's schoolfriend, by the hand. Charlotte looked miserable, like usual, and pale as a ghost in a silver chiffon dress.

"No, Mama," she muttered.

"These men and their vile cigarettes," Mrs. Cartwright said. "We should go back to the dancing."

"If only they hadn't hired a jazz band. So vulgar..."

Much to Jess's relief, they finally took poor Charlotte and wandered away and left her alone again. She stretched out her legs under the handkerchief hem of her pink satin Poiret bridesmaid's gown, and settled in to enjoy her ciggie in peace.

Peace didn't last very long.

"There you are, you horrid thing!"

At the sound of that loud cry, Jess felt a rush of panic that her mother had found her, She tried to stub out the cigarette, and whirled around, an excuse on her lips—only to find her best friend, Lady Margaret Montley, standing there.

Meggie's hands were planted on her hips as she gave Jess a mock glare. As usual, her wild golden curls were sliding from their jeweled combs, and her fashionably straight blue silk gown couldn't contain her unfashionably voluptuous figure. Meggie never cared at all that she wasn't in style; she was always unabashedly herself. It was the reason they had become immediate and fast pals at Mrs. Greensley's School For Young Ladies.

"Meggie, you gave me a heart seizure," Jess said. "I thought you were Mum."

"She did look as if she was searching for you, but then David made her dance with him, so you're safe for a few minutes. I saw poor Charlotte Leighton being dragged away her mother. Here, scoot over so I can hide, too," Meggie said.

Jess slid over in the little hollow behind the tree, and dug around in her beaded purse for her silver cigarette case and lighter. She lit up one for each of them, and they smoked in companionable silence for a long moment. The shadows of evening were creeping in, making the lights of the Chinese lanterns in the tents glow brighter, the music of the horns and the drums louder.

"Was that old Mrs. Cartwright I saw wandering away with Charlotte and her mother?" Meggie said.

"Mm-hm," Jessica answered. She tucked the short strands of her red-gold bob behind her ears. "She and her horrid old bosom bow. They were dreadful about David's scars."

"I doubt he would care one jot," Meggie said with a snort. "He and your sister looked heavenly happy. And we won't have to worry about the likes of them anymore either. Do you have it with you?"

Jessica laughed. "Of course I do! I carry it with me everywhere, so I can remind myself it's almost time." She opened her purse again and found the tickets carefully folded and tucked in the bottom.

They each bent closer to read the precious words. The Cunard Line—*Empress of India*—departing Southampton for New York City. One first class cabin, two berths, for

Jess and Meggie. Or rather, for their alter egos Miss Hampton and Mrs. Mortley.

"I can't believe it!" Meggie whispered in excitement. "Only a fortnight away."

"And then we'll be in New York!" Jess could hardly believe it herself. In only a few weeks, she would be away from England, away from her mother trying to force her into being the perfect deb, and wandering the glittering streets of New York. America. Sparkling high-rise windows, stretching all the way to the sky. Jazz, and shops, and taxis—and freedom.

"It will be even more fun than the time we put glue in the locks on finals day at Mrs. Greensley's. But are you sure they'll hire you once they see you're—well, not exactly what they're expecting?" Meggie said.

"Of course," Jess said, with a confidence she didn't quite feel bone-deep. But she would have to make herself feel it, very soon. Confidence would carry her through. "They just want some plummy-sounding British aristocrat. A lady is as good as a lord when it comes to a byline. And I never *told* them I was a man."

She'd just signed her letter of application as JEO Hatton of Hatton Hall, Surrey. If they didn't think that meant Jessica Elizabeth Olivia Hatton, tough nuts to them. They'd liked her sample articles, and she would knock their socks off with what she could write there.

She was going to be a real, true-life newspaper writer. That was all that mattered.

"Come on," she said, putting out her cigarette. "Mum will be looking for us. We can't give her any cause for suspicion, not if we're going to pull this off."

"Oh, we'll pull it off all right," Meggie said with her usual confidence. "I'm not missing out on America for anything."

They hugged in a sudden burst of exuberant giggles. It *was* going to happen! The adventure they had schemed and planned for ever since they were at school. It was finally coming true...

One

Aboard the *Empress of India*

"DO YOU SMELL THAT, Meggie?" Jessica cried as she leaned into the cold, salt spray wind, her t-strap shoes perched on the lowest rung of the ship's railing. She'd lost her hat, and the short strands of her hair blew into her eyes, but she didn't care. England was far behind them. They had escaped.

"It smells like freedom!" she shouted, and threw up her arms. It felt like she could fly all the way to America.

"I only smell old fish," Meggie said. "Now come down from there, Jess. If you tumble into the drink, it will all be over before it even starts."

Jessica laughed and shook her head, but she did climb down. She spun around to see Meggie stretched out on one of the deck chairs, the glossy mink collar of her coat drawn close around her.

The sky *was* grey and dismal-looking, the water not as glassy-smooth as when they slid past Ireland yesterday and headed out to open sea. Several of the passengers had retreated to their cabins, but Jessica couldn't stand staying inside. Not when there was so much to be seen.

"It smells like fish *and* freedom," Jessica insisted. "But we can go in now. Maybe Charlotte and Eliza will want to play some cards or mah-jong."

"Finally," Meggie grumbled as she swung her feet down to the damp deck. But her smile was broad. Jessica knew Meggie was loving it all just as much as she was.

"Come on, let's find Charlotte and Eliza," Jessica said, racing ahead toward the ship's salon. Their adventure had started growing on the boat train from London, when they met their old schoolmate Charlotte Leighton, and heard her romantic tale of fleeing an arranged marriage. So Victorian and tragic! They persuaded her to change her booking to their own ship.

And when they decided they should find a phony "lady's maid," to appear respectable and deflect suspicion, they found the perfect candidate on the docks in the person of Eliza Gilbert. A pretty ex-housemaid, she had been turned out of her position when her employer's evil son tried to seduce her.

Jessica made sure to take copious notes. If journalism didn't work out, surely she could turn to novel writing! The four of them were going to have to support themselves somehow. The running-away money she had saved for years wouldn't last much longer.

Meggie caught up with her, and hand in hand they ran toward the salon, laughing as they waved at some of the handsome sailors.

"Coming to the fancy dress party tonight, ladies?" one of them called.

"Wouldn't miss it for the world!" Jessica answered. Fancy dress parties were one of her very favorite things—and one at sea was bound to be doubly fun.

She swung around the corner, only to almost knock over the lady standing outside the glass salon doors. They skidded on the slippery wooden deck, and Meggie had to grab both their arms to keep them from falling.

"I'm so sorry," Jessica gasped, dizzy. She saw it was the petite, delicate—and quite mysterious—Countess Markova she had almost barreled into. The lady was swathed in pale furs, a satin turban over her hair, and a tiny white dog under her arm.

"*Nyet*," the countess said, waving a gloved hand. "Is—how you say? Nothing."

Jessica and Meggie exchanged a glance. The countess, obviously a Russian noblewoman cruelly cast out of her homeland by the Bolsheviks, had been an object of intense speculation for Jessica and her friends ever since they saw her come aboard. They all had ideas about what her dramatic story could be, but the lady herself was elusive. They only caught glimpses of her around the ship.

Like now. Jessica watched, fascinated, as the countess drifted away along the deck. At the railing, she took the arm of a tall man in a black overcoat and stylish black, broad-brimmed hat. He turned to smile down at her—and Jessica almost gasped.

It was quite shocking how good-looking he was. Surely men like that only existed in the cinema. Jessica was used to pale-faced, stammering boys from "good families" who steered her clumsily around the floor at tea dances and yammered on about cricket.

She would bet this man *never* talked about cricket. And that he could dance a wicked tango.

His profile under the brim of his hat was sharply cut, all elegant angles, his strong jaw roughened with whiskers as dark as his wavy black hair. Like a marble statue of some Roman god in a museum, only alive. Dark and vibrant.

Jessica shivered just looking at him.

"Good heavens! Do you suppose that's Ramon Novarro?" Meggie whispered, making Jessica break into giggles. They had just seen Novarro's movie *Thy Name is Woman* before they left England, and everyone had enormous crushes on him.

The countess and her stunning companion looked back at them at the sudden burst of noise. Jessica had a glimpse of wintery, sea-blue eyes, and suddenly she couldn't breathe. She felt so embarrassed, like a stupid little schoolgirl gawking at an actorly crush on the stage, yet neither could she turn away.

His smile widened, as if he knew what she was thinking, and Jessica whirled around. She grabbed Meggie's arm and dragged her into the salon.

"I wasn't done staring," Meggie said with a laugh.

"I thought we were going to find the others and play mah-jong or something," Jessica snapped.

Meggie gave her a puzzled look, but she knew better than to say anything. She shrugged. "Sure. Sounds like fun. I'll grab a table, you go and find them."

Jessica spun around and rushed away, not quite sure where she was actually going. She just knew she *had* to get away from the glamorous countess's companion before she dissolved into a puddle of blushes and giggles, like all those silly girls she and Meggie went to Mrs. Greensley's School with, and who she wanted to forget. She was starting a brand-new, grown-up life in a new city, no more silly English missishness!

She ran up a narrow flight of stairs, rolling slightly with the waves of the ship, and along a corridor. Two passing sailors called out cheerful greetings as she hurried past.

"Still coming to the fancy dress party?" one said, as did everyone who had seen her that day. The party was all she could think about, until she saw the countess's matinee idol friend.

"Of course," she answered with a laugh. "I'm counting on you for my costume, don't forget."

"How could we forget *that*?" the sailor said with a wink, making her laugh even harder. He was handsome, with blond curls and broad shoulders, and like all his mates was fun company to play cards and shuffleboard with on the long voyage. Yet when he teased her, flirted with her, it didn't make her even a fraction as flustered as one look from "Ramon Novarro."

She gave the sailors a jaunty wave and hurried on to the cabin she and Meggie now shared with Eliza and Charli at the end of the corridor. She had to shove hard at the door since someone's hatbox was in the way, and inside the same scene of chaos she'd left a few hours ago greeted her.

The four narrow bunks were unmade and strewn with dresses and silky slips and combinations, with shoes shoved underneath haphazardly. Pots of lotions and tubes of lipsticks were scattered across the one table bolted beneath the small porthole.

In the meager, greyish light that came in through the thick glass, Jessica saw that Charli hadn't left her bunk. She was huddled underneath her blankets, her nose buried in a book. Her carrot-red hair, brighter than Jessica's strawberry, which they had persuaded her to bob with Eliza's sewing scissors, was tousled, her spectacles perched on the end of her nose.

Eliza stood at the small basin, rinsing out a shirtwaist. The smell of Persil soap, flowery and rich, hung in the stuffy air.

"Eliza, we told you—no more washing up! You aren't really our maid." Jessica stamped across the cabin to tug the blankets off Charlotte's knees. "It's a lovely day outside. Come up on deck and play mah-jong with us."

"Horsefeathers! I just need to get out this one spot..." Eliza muttered.

"And I need to finish this chapter!" Charli argued.

"No, and no." The cabin was so small Jessica could snatch away both the wet shirtwaist and the book with only two steps. "It's time for fun now. Come on!"

Charli still tried to protest, fun being so new to her, but Eliza got into the spirit of things and caught the book from Jessica's hand to keep it away from her.

"Mah-jong, and no more arguments!" Jessica cried, twirling away. "In half an hour, in the salon."

Before anyone could make another protest, she skipped out into the corridor and slammed the cabin door behind her. The narrow hallways were deserted now, all the crew off on their duties and all the passengers resting up for the fancy dress party. All that silence, the roll of the carpeted floor beneath her feet, the faint, far-away roar of the ship's engines, made her feel restless again. Giddy. She took off running, leaping up the stairs in exactly the way her mother had always scolded her not to.

She swung around a corner—and almost tripped to a sudden standstill. The devastatingly handsome man she saw with the countess earlier stood near the railing, talking with another man, one in the uniform of a crew's officer.

There was nothing wrong with that, of course. Jessica talked to the ship's crew all the time. But she didn't know this officer at all, and something about *that* man, the matinee idol in all his silver-screenish glory, made her freeze in her headlong dash. She slowly backed up and ducked around the corner before they could spot her.

She carefully peeked at them, wishing she could hear what they were saying. The crew member had his back to her, but she could see the handsome stranger's profile under the brim of his hat. There was a darkly intent look on his chiseled features, a tautness that almost looked like barely leashed—anger. His hand, with its long, elegant fingers, was curled into a fist on the railing.

One of the reasons Jessica wanted to be a reporter so badly was the simple fact that people were so fascinating, and so—so *weird*. Ever since she was a kid, she carried around a notebook to jot down things people said or did that she could puzzle over and decipher later. She loved hearing people's stories, discovering their secrets.

And she would bet that "Ramon Novarro" over there had a doozy.

She stared, watching as the two men went on talking in low, barely coherent voices, words that were snatched away on the sea breeze. Their glances between themselves were not what she would call friendly, either. What could be going on there?

Jeepers, but she wished she had her notebook with her!

Just as her neck was starting to get sore from craning around the corner, the crew member gave an abrupt nod and stalked away. She had a quick glimpse of his craggy, bearded face as he passed her hidey-hole, and he definitely looked angry. Angry and, astonishingly, scared. Scared of what? Her mind raced with all sorts of wonderfully lurid possibilities. Gambling debts. Rum-running. Blackmail. Quarrels over a beautiful showgirl.

No, not a showgirl. Not for "Ramon Novarro," surely. She didn't like that thought at all.

"You can come out from there now, if you like. It can't be very comfortable pressed up to the wall like that," the matinee idol suddenly said. He spoke quietly, calmly, but his faintly accented voice carried to her all too well on the salty wind. He sounded amused.

To her shame, she felt a hot blush flare across her face to be caught eavesdropping like that, and by *him* of all people. But really, who was he to make her feel like a chastened child about to be sent to bed with no supper? She was Lady Jessica Hatton, daughter of an earl, and a soon-to-be famous reporter, too.

She stood up so ramrod-straight her old deportment teacher at Mrs. Greensley's would be proud, tossed her head back, and marched out of her hiding place. He glanced over his shoulder at her, and she saw that the corners of his mouth looked as if he was just about to smile, but other than that he didn't look as if he moved at all.

And up-close she saw he was even more breathtakingly handsome. The real Ramon Novarro should worry about losing his job to pale blue eyes and cheekbones that could cut glass.

"I didn't want to interrupt what looked like a private conversation," she said haughtily, trying to mimic her mother's best "countess" tone. She felt totally ridiculous, though.

What was it about this man that made her feel so wrong-footed? All those debutante balls, tea dances, even curtsying to the queen, should have knocked shyness out of her.

He turned to fully face her, and that tiny, secret smile turned into a full-blown grin that almost knocked her back a step it was so gorgeous.

"I should go," she said, the "countess" voice totally gone. "My friends are waiting."

She spun around, away from the sight of him, but it was no good. She could still feel him watching her with those pale, sea-colored eyes. That smile.

"Are you coming to the dance tonight?" he called, and she suddenly recognized that accent. It sounded Russian, like all the refugees from the Revolution who had flooded into London's ballrooms in the last couple of years. That only made him even more intriguing, damn him.

"I shall have to check my calendar. It is rather full at the moment," she said airily, rather proud of how calm she sounded now.

He ruined all that by laughing. *Laughing!* Even worse, his laughter sounded delicious, like the slide of a first sip of fizzy champagne.

She dashed away, but even as she ducked into the salon like it was her last sanctuary, closing her eyes against the day, she could still hear that laughter in her mind. That accent...

"Jeepers, Jess, but what happened to you?" Meggie cried. "You look like a ghost chased you down the deck."

Jessica opened her eyes to see her friends were all gathered around the table already, the mah-jong tiles spread in front of them. They all stared up at her curiously, Charli squinting a little without her specs.

Flustered, Jessica pushed herself away from the door and shook her skirt back into place. She would probably tell them all about the Russian matinee idol, but not now. Tonight, in their cabin, when it was dark and she didn't feel so horribly shaken-up. When she could think rationally about the mystery of him.

For now, though, he was just her little secret.

"I just took a wrong turn belowdecks and got lost," she said with a laugh. "Come on, are we playing mah-jong or not?"

Durak! Nicolai Dimitriovich Romanov-Markov, now known by everyone as Frank Markov, watched the redheaded sprite of a girl dash away like a bright butterfly in the gray day. He had seen her before, standing on the ship's railing with her arms flung out as if she would fly, and racing around the decks laughing with her friends. It had made him laugh, too, just to see the sheer, raw exuberance of her. Had he ever been that young? He didn't think so anymore.

And it had been far too long since he laughed at anything at all.

Frank turned away from the sight of her, and rubbed his hand hard over the back of his neck as he muttered another curse. With her bright hair and vivid spirit, she reminded him too much of another such shining spirit. A girl who once spun through the gilded ballrooms of St. Petersburg, drawing him out onto palm-shielded verandas with her laughter and the scent of gardenias in her hair. Before she sent him off to war with just such a flower pressed into his hand.

But that girl was long-gone now, along with all of his old life in Russia. He couldn't afford to lose himself in this woman's radiance, no matter how deeply tempted he was to run after her now. To demand to know her name, to make her tell him what she laughed at. She was obviously a lady, with her fine accent and manners, despite her bobbed hair and free laughter.

He had a mission now, and where he was going no one could follow. Especially not aristocratic butterfly girls like that red-head.

"Did you speak to him?" someone said suddenly in Russian.

Frank turned to see his aunt, the Countess Markova, as she was now known, standing at the railing behind him. That she had been able to creep up on him like that was another bad sign of his distraction. Her beautiful face smiled, but he saw the hardness behind it.

"He will do it," Frank answered in the same language. In that instant of coming face-to-face with the laughing girl, he'd almost forgotten why they were on the *Empress of India* in the first place. The mission that had taken them from Siberia to Paris and London, and now to New York, where they would finally end things. Finally have their revenge.

He wouldn't forget again.

A brittle smile curved the countess's pretty, pink-rouged mouth, but her ice-blue eyes were flat and opaque. "Excellent. The more allies we can find the better."

"Allies? Or mere greedy minions?" he said with a bark of humorless laughter.

"Does it matter? As long as they are useful to us." She took a step closer to him and laid her gloved hand on his arm. Her touch was light, but in it he felt all the iron weight of their past. The blood-stained snow. The screams.

"You have surely not lost your resolve?" she said.

"*Nyet*," he answered brusquely. "I will never forget. You know that."

"Good. Not when we are so close to the end."

She tugged at his arm, and he let her lead him toward the smoking salon. She was right. The end, which they had schemed and plotted and killed for, was finally within sight. He would never give it up for anything. He had vowed that to his lost family.

But he couldn't help one glance back, just to see if there was still one last glimpse of strawberry-red hair. But she was gone.

http://amandamccabe.com

Ruined

Alicia Dean

One

The Earl of Goodwin's Country Estate, Abbots Langley, England, 1924

"YOU MUST FLEE, MY child." Maud's gaze darted around the kitchen of the main house, then returned to Eliza. "T'isn't safe for you here."

Eliza Gilbert gently patted Maud's arthritic hands. "Please don't fret, Maud. I can take care of myself." The woman had been like a mother to her since her own mum passed away just over a year ago. Maud had no husband, no children. Eliza was the closest to family she had. "I don't want to leave you. Besides, I have nowhere to go." Eliza tried to keep the hitch out of her voice. She didn't wish to upset Maud further, but the awful truth was, she *truly* had nowhere else to go. Was she destined to be a housemaid like her mum for the rest of her life? *Or worse…*

Worry over Eliza deepened the grooves in Maud's worn features. "But Lord Renwald will be home soon. You promised your mum, God rest her soul, that once the old Earl passed, you would leave." She flitted her free hand to her heart. "The Earl, God rest his soul, was the only thing standing betwixt you and the lord's lechery."

Lord Renwald had been leering at Eliza since she'd turned twelve and started to develop breasts. When she was fifteen, he'd cornered her in the stable, and no telling what might have happened if James, the stable boy, hadn't come to her rescue. Even now, a knot of revulsion clogged her throat at the memory of Lord Renwald's greedy hands on her body. After that, the Earl had kept a close eye on his son when the viscount was home from Oxford. But now the Earl was gone, along with her protection.

Eliza offered Maud a reassuring smile. "I can take care of myself. Rest assured, I'll be no man's tart."

"When Lord Renwald arrives, I'm afraid you won't have a choice." Maud glanced around the kitchen again before lowering her voice. "I've packed a valise for you should you need to leave in a rush. You'll find it in the cubby beneath the stairs. I've also tucked a few pounds in the pocket." Tears surfaced in her kind brown eyes. "I hope it never comes to that, but should you need to flee, you take that and run. And never look back."

Eliza pushed aside the worry Maud's words evoked. Granted, the man had been a plague on her life since childhood, but surely he would not be so bold as to force the issue. She would simply make it clear that she intended to remain on as part of the staff. Anything more was out of the question.

"I will, I promise. As I said, I can handle him." She wished she were as confident as she proclaimed, but worrying Maud would not help matters. "Now, let's see to polishing the staircase banister shall we?"

Two days later, Lord Renwald returned to the estate. He hadn't troubled to attend his father's funeral, but he was back to claim his inheritance. With Maud's help, Eliza succeeded in staying out of his way the entire day. She breathed a sigh of relief when suppertime came and went and she hadn't run into him. Once her tasks were completed, she headed to her room in the attic. Just before she reached the top of the stairs, Miles, one of the footmen, approached.

"Eliza, the master has requested your presence in the study." Miles' features showed concern, but his tone remained level.

Eliza swallowed the apprehensive flutter that darted from her heart to her throat. "Why does he wish to see me?"

"I am afraid I do not know." But his failure to look her in the eyes indicated he did, just as she did.

Eliza nodded. "Thank you, Miles."

With lead feet, she made her way to the study. She smoothed her dull brown uniform skirt with trembling fingers, then knocked timidly, a foolish part of her hoping he wouldn't hear.

"Come in."

She drew in a fortifying breath and opened the door. Lord Renwald stood in front of the fireplace, a snifter of dark amber liquid in his hand, one booted foot propped on the marble hearth. He was tall and thin, reminding her of an ostrich the way he always strutted around with his chin jutted forward.

"You wished to see me, my lord?"

The viscount stretched his thick lips into a self-satisfied grin. "Yes, do come in. Close the door."

She hesitated for a moment, then did as he bade.

His gaze ran over her body. "No sense beating around the bush. I believe you've been aware of my…interest in you for quite some time."

She crossed her hands in front of her and tightened her lips but didn't respond.

"I have a new position for you. You will no longer toil as a housemaid. Instead, I shall take you as my mistress." His tone indicated he'd offered her a rare gift.

She refrained from releasing the mocking laughter bubbling inside. "Thank you for the offer, my lord, but I respectfully decline."

His eyes widened. "Decline, do you? Perhaps you misunderstood. My statement was not a request. You *will* become my mistress." He stalked toward her, and Eliza took a step back.

"No, I will not. I shall leave my employment here altogether before I agree to become your mistress."

He threw his head back and laughed. "While I find your coyness delightful, my patience is wearing thin." He finished off his drink and slammed the glass down on a nearby table with a sharp crack like a gunshot. He strode to her and grabbed her shoulders. Yanking her against his body, he pressed wet, thick lips on her mouth.

Bile surfaced in her throat, and she gagged, jerking away from him and wiping her mouth.

He glared down at her. His muddy brown eyes sparked fire just before he slapped her cheek so hard, her ears rang.

Tears sprang to her eyes, but she turned back to him, lifting her chin and staring into his hateful face. "Release me this instant." In spite of the stinging in her cheek and her fear of what else he might be capable of, she forced bravado into her tone. "I hereby resign."

Rage suffused his narrow cheeks with red. "You stupid chit. You dare to defy *me*?" He gripped a handful of her hair and jerked her head back. "I shall have you. And when I am finished, you will be out on the streets. But not until I say, do you understand?" Without giving her a chance to respond, he once more forced his mouth on hers. His grip on her hair brought fresh tears in her eyes and set her scalp on fire. He grabbed the front of her uniform blouse and yanked. Cool air hit her exposed breasts. Panic threatened to choke her.

He was going to rape her. If she didn't do something now, he was going to have his way with her. Nausea and terror clamped her stomach. A haze filled her mind, and all she could think was, *I'm going to die, I'm going to die…*

Desperation spurring her, she reached out to the side table. Her fingers closed around the neck of a crystal vase. With a cry, she hefted the urn and slammed it into the back of Lord Renwald's head. Flowers spewed into the air, droplets of water sprinkling her face.

Lord Renwald bellowed, then fell to his knees, one hand on his head, blood seeping between his fingers. His mouth gaped like a fish, his eyes wide and agony-filled. He reached his free hand for her and nearly gripped her skirt, but she jumped back, out of his reach. He frowned as if perplexed, then thudded to the floor—still as a corpse.

Eliza stood frozen for a moment. Her entire body trembled. Warm stickiness coated her fingers. She'd killed a man. Not just a man, but an Earl. Dear Heaven, she'd *killed* him. If they caught her, she'd be put to death. The realization jolted her from her trance. She dropped the vase and rushed to the door, flinging it open. She raced down the hallway, to the stairs that led to the lower floor. Nearly flying, she hurried down the steps, past the wide-eyed stares of the other housemaids, and opened the cubby. Just as Maud promised, the valise was inside. Eliza snatched it and rushed to the back door. Her heart ached that she hadn't had a chance to tell Maud goodbye, to thank her. But she'd promised the woman she would run and never look back. She didn't know where she would go, or how she would get there, but she knew she would never return.

Two

Manhattan, New York, Six Months Later

ELIZA BUTTONED AN EMERALD green jacket over her yellow drop-waist dress. The weather was balmy for October, and she would prefer to shed the jacket altogether, but she couldn't seek employment with the frayed sleeves of her dress showing. She *must* land this position. Her purse held all the money she had in the world—five dollars, her final pay from the garment factory. Two days had passed since she'd been let go, but she hadn't yet found the nerve to tell her flatmates. Jess and Charli and Meggie had done so much for her from the moment they met on the docks, through their travels, and setting up in New York. It was time she stood on her own and repaid them.

She pushed open the diner door, jingling a bell hanging above. The sign outside stated they had need of a counter girl. The position probably did not pay as much as the factory, but she had to find employment—soon.

The smell of frying meat filled the air, making her stomach rumble. She approached the counter. A middle-aged man with a receding hairline and a cigar stub protruding from his mouth narrowed his eyes at her. The name badge on his stained apron read Frederick. "Can I help you, miss?"

"Yes, please." Her stomach growled again, and her face warmed. Hopefully, he hadn't heard. She was famished. The last thing she'd eaten was one of Charli's cinnamon scones that morning. Her mouth watered at the thought of the warm, flaky, delicious pastries. Why hadn't she eaten two? She swallowed. "I've come to inquire about the position as counter girl. I'm a hard worker and a fast learner. I'd make you a fine employee."

He frowned. "Sorry, the position is filled." His eyes dropped away. He was lying. She'd told enough fibs to recognize when others were doing the same.

"But, sir. Your sign is still up. Are you certain the position has been filled?"

With a grunt, he plucked the cigar from his mouth and pointed it at her. "Okay, truth is, the position's still open. But you ain't getting it. I don't want no dame with a limey accent greetin' my customers."

She blinked in surprise. In all the months she'd been in America, she'd been treated well. Truly believed she'd found the land of opportunity. She'd never forget her first glimpse of the Statue of Liberty. Her heart had swelled with happiness and hope. At that moment, she'd felt anything was possible. This man's prejudice was not indicative of the attitude of most Americans she'd met. She had no desire to work with an oaf such as this, but she was desperate.

"Please, sir. I can disguise my accent." She attempted to erase the British inflection as she said the words, but even to her ears, she was unsuccessful. "I need work, and I promise you won't regret it." Before he could deny her a second time, she rushed on, "Or I can cook. Wash dishes. Anything you need. In London, I was head of the entire kitchen staff." Not quite the truth, but it was unlikely he would check her references all the way in England. Besides, she'd killed her former boss, so there would be no one to give her a poor review. "You won't regret it, I promise."

"Sorry, doll. I only need a counter girl. And you can't disguise your accent. You sound about as American as Mussolini. Now scram. I got work to do."

She drew in a breath, ready to launch into an argument, but the set of his features and the clenching of his fists told her the words would be useless. And she didn't want to make any more of a fool of herself than she already had.

Eyes down, she hurried past the occupants in the diner. Stepping outside, she hiccupped back tears. Dusk was settling over the city, along with the smell of exhaust from the vehicles clogging the streets. She headed down the crowded sidewalk, barely aware of the bleeping horns and chatter of pedestrians. Her brain fogged with worry. What now?

How much longer could she pretend to leave for work each morning, while in reality walking the streets of New York City, searching for a job? She would certainly have to confess the truth to her friends when her meager funds ran out.

She pulled out her clutch and unlatched the clasp. The paltry five dollars inside mocked her. Three of that would be taken by her share of the rent, due tomorrow. Only two dollars left to last until she not only found a position, but received her first week's pay. And judging from her job search the past few days, it was certain to be a while before something surfaced. If it ever did. She suppressed the urge to weep. What would she do?

Just as she clasped the latch on her purse, a force jarred her from behind, slamming her to the walk. She fell to her knee, instinctively thrusting her hands in front of her. Her clutch skittered away. Cement scraped the flesh on her palms, and stinging agony shot through her wrists to her shoulders. She choked back a sob and came to her feet just in time to see a man in a brown shirt, fedora low over his eyes snatch up her clutch and take off running.

"Hey!" She started after him, but the pain in her knee impeded her progress. A few passersby shot curious looks, but moved on without offering assistance. The thief disappeared around a corner. She halted, breathing heavily. "Bloody fig!" The words came out more as a sob than the angry insult she intended. She stomped her foot, causing another wave of pain to shoot through her body. Holding out her bleeding, scraped hands, she assessed the damage. Her palms throbbed like hell, but she was so angry she was certain she wasn't feeling the pain as much as she would when her adrenaline ebbed.

"Bloody horsefeathers. *Damn, damn, damnation.*"

Her mother would have told her maybe the poor bloke needed it worse than she did, but her mother was addle-brained if she believed that, God rest her soul. The chances he needed it more than she did were slim. Even if he did, that was of no consequence. It was *her* money. She'd sweated and poked her fingers with those bloody sewing needles for a solid week to earn that. And now look at her. Where had it gotten her? Was her fate in Abbots Langley more desirable than the one she now faced?

No, no it wasn't. Not only would she have been at Lord Renwald's lecherous mercy, in Abbots Langley she had no one other than Maud. And Maud was getting on in years. Eliza had lost her mum and the Earl. Once Maud was gone, she would have no one. In New York, she had friends—sisters, really.

At the thought of the girls, panic leapt to her throat. That was all the cash she had. Rent was due. She had no job. How would she face her flatmates? More than just flatmates, they were her friends. They'd found her on the docks, included her on their journey to America on the *Empress of India*—they'd *saved* her. She'd posed as their lady's maid, and the ship's steward had allowed all four girls to board without raising a brow. They'd all been running from something, though none of them from a murder they'd committed, as was she. She hadn't confessed the incident with Lord Renwald. She'd only told the girls she was leaving the employ of a tyrant boss. It was the partial truth at least, and thank Heaven, they'd believed her. Trusted her. *What a bunch of saps*. If they knew the real her…

No matter how much she tried, she wasn't like the other girls. They'd come from wealthy, loving homes. They had already found opportunity here in the land of the free. And she had been nothing but a failure.

"Hey, Miss, are you okay?"

She whirled at the sound of a male voice, for one second foolishly believing her attacker had suffered a bout of conscience and come to return the money. But this man was not the one who had mugged her. The crook had been slight of build. The man standing in front of her was tall and wide. He wore a brown pinstriped suit with a dark gold vest underneath. His stomach protruded through a gap between the buttons. His brown hair was sparse on top, combed to the side to try and take advantage of the small amount he still possessed. She frowned. The man looked familiar. Where had she seen him before?

She wasn't certain, but she had more important things on her mind at the moment. She had to find a way to come up with money—fast. And find a job—immediately. Yeah, fat chance of either of those happening. She drew in a deep breath and wiped the back of her hand over her brow. "I'm fine. Just a little scuffed up. That…cad…stole my pocket book."

"Yes, I heard your…*opinion* of the thief." Amusement lit his eyes.

Heat flooded her cheeks. So he'd heard her swearing like a fishwife? "Yes, well—"

"Don't worry. I don't blame you. In your position, I might have said worse."

She cast her eyes down. "It's just that…I only this moment…obtained a job at the diner. I needed that money to get by until I received my pay."

"You're saying you were hired at the diner?"

She lifted her head. Something in his expression told her he knew she was lying. How? Then it dawned on her. He looked familiar because he'd been one of the customers inside. *Horsefeathers*. He'd heard her humiliation with the owner, and now this?

"Yes. Um, I really must be getting home now. If you'll pardon me." She started down the sidewalk, but his voice stopped her.

"Wait. You're hurt. Let me take you to the hospital."

She paused and looked back at him. "No, thank you. It's only a few scrapes. I'm almost home." In truth, she was quite a distance from home. She'd traveled over fifteen blocks in her job search. She didn't relish the idea of walking back on an injured knee. But she also didn't relish the thought of being accosted by a bounder.

He offered a smile. "I understand why you wouldn't trust me. You don't know me. But I've seen you before. At The Globe Theater, right?"

She nodded slowly. "My friend, Meggie, is an actress who performs there."

"Lady Margaret, of course. My name is Oscar Cummings. I have a regular box at the theater."

Ah, yes. She'd seen him there a few times. But she was also certain he'd been in the diner. "Right. Mr. Cummings. I remember. Nice to see you again, but really, I must be going."

"Please." He took her arm in a gentle grip. "My car is right here." He pointed to a black sedan. "I live nearby. If you won't go to the hospital, at least let me take you to my apartment where I have salve and bandages to treat your wounds. You shouldn't walk home in this condition."

He was right. Her hands stung as though fire ants feasted on her flesh. Her knees throbbed, and it took every ounce of willpower not to burst into tears. A ride in an automobile sounded so much more appealing than limping fifteen blocks home. But going to the apartment of a strange man? No, not wise. She'd learned her lesson from Lord Renwald.

She shook her head. "No need. I'm not far from home. Thank you for your kind offer."

"Of course." He bowed at the waist. "If you're certain you're okay, I'll leave you. However, I fear my gentlemanly conscience will be sorely vexed." He wiped at his eyes. Were those…tears? He gave an embarrassed laugh. "Forgive me my sentimentality. You remind me of my niece, and the thought of her wandering the streets injured, unattended…"

She stood indecisively. He most definitely seemed harmless. And he was so concerned. He was a regular at the theater…

And Lord Renwald had been the son of a kind man she knew and trusted. Yet she couldn't trust *him* as far as she could toss him.

"Thank you, but no." She turned her back and took two steps. Pain shot from her knee to her thigh, her leg crumpled, and she nearly fell again. Blast! Frustrated tears fought to surface, but she would not cry…

"Miss, please. Let me help you."

Her knee hurt too badly to think clearly. Making it home in this condition would be painful, if not impossible. Her instincts had sharpened during her time on the streets before she'd met the girls. She knew in her gut, this man was not a blackguard. He was more like the Earl than Lord Renwald. Biting her lip to stem the tears, she nodded. "On second thought, your help would be appreciated, Mr. Cummings."

Worry melted from his face, replaced by relief. "Splendid." He held the door open for her, and she slipped inside, then settled against the seat.

He climbed into the driver's side, and the vehicle bumped along the streets, passing pedestrians at nearly ten times their speed. Eliza let out a contented sigh. This was the only way to get around. Someday, maybe she would have one of her own.

"What kind of automobile is this?" She tried to keep the envy out of her voice.

"A Jordan Brougham. I own a Nash as well, but I prefer the Jordan. It's a much smoother ride."

"It's beautiful."

He shot her a smile and, in a few moments, pulled next to a curb in front of a building that was at least twenty floors high. Inside, he escorted her across a mosaic-patterned carpet in black and gray tones that was as plush as cotton.

They stepped off the elevator on the twentieth floor. Nervously, she followed. She hadn't seen anything this fancy since the estate in Abbots Langley. And there she'd been a mere servant. Here, she was a guest. Her stomach no longer rumbled with hunger, it was too filled with apprehension.

He stopped before double wooden doors and fitted his key in the lock, then swung the door open. She remained rooted in the hallway until he said, "Please, come in. It's fine."

With a hesitant step, she was inside. She looked around, unable to stop a small gasp from escaping her lips. The room was as opulent as any at the Earl's estate. Rich golden draperies hung over floor length windows. In the center of the room sat a sofa with a matching settee and chair covered in ivory satin and trimmed in gold. The décor was elegant and luxurious without being vulgar.

"Your home is lovely."

Mr. Cummings smiled. "Thank you. Have a seat, and I'll get some salve and bandages."

Eliza eyed the sofa warily. She would not sit on such a glorious item and make a mess of it. "I can stand."

"Nonsense. Sit." He prodded with a gentle hand to her back until she lowered gingerly onto the edge of the sofa. "I'll be right back."

In moments, he returned, carrying a first aid kit and a glass of water. He sat next to her and placed the kit on the gleaming oak coffee table. Retrieving a bottle of aspirin, he shook out two and handed them to her, along with the water. She swallowed the aspirin, and he took the glass from her, setting it on a side table. He removed bandages and antiseptic salve. "Give me your hands." She did, and he rested them, palms up, on his knees. He offered a reassuring smile. "This won't hurt much, I promise."

She released the breath she'd had pent up in her chest. He was so kind, just the type of man she imagined her father would have been had he lived. He'd died in a farming accident when she was an infant. She had no recollection of him at all—only the locket with a small photo of his mustached, smiling image she wore around her neck—but when she was small, she'd fantasized about what he was like. Oscar Cummings was so close to a fantasy father, it was eerie.

"There, all done."

She blinked and looked down. Her hands were bandaged, the pain had ebbed, and she'd barely been aware of his ministrations.

"Thank you. Really. You're much too kind."

He chuckled. "Nonsense, my dear. I'm pleased I could help."

She rose from the sofa, unsure of what to do next. She couldn't very well ask him for a ride home after all his kindness, but his penthouse was five miles or so from The Gables Boardinghouse where she lived. She couldn't walk that distance in the dark. And she hadn't the funds for a taxi. Letting him know of her troubles was out of the question. He'd heard enough of her complaints. With an uncertain laugh, she said, "Now, I must be off. Thank you again."

"Let me see you home. You can't go wandering the streets after dark."

Relief swept through her. "That's very kind of you."

He narrowed his eyes as if in thought and put a finger to his lips. "Now that I think about it, perhaps I can offer you something more than a bandage and a ride home."

Her interest piqued, she lifted her brows. "Such as?"

"I am aware you…uh… just landed a new job, but I might have a position for you. Something I think you'll enjoy more. One that pays *much* better."

Hope lit inside her, but she attempted not to appear too anxious. "What kind of position would that be?"

"I need a hostess. Someone to help me with parties."

"Parties?" A position that paid for assisting with parties? Who'd ever heard of such a thing? "You would like to hire me to plan parties?"

"Not plan parties. More like a hostess. I need someone to help me by mingling with my guests. The job pays twenty-five dollars a week."

She nearly gasped aloud. Had she heard him correctly? Surely she was in a dream. Her salary at the factory had been five dollars per week, but once they deducted monies as reimbursement for what they considered mistakes—a crooked stitch, a bent needle, or any other minor misstep—she was lucky to come home with half that. "You would pay me to attend parties?"

"Yes. People love to have fun, and they enjoy having beautiful girls around them at parties. And you are quite beautiful."

Her cheeks warmed at the compliment. Excitement brimmed at his proposal. Everything in her screamed, *'Take the job, you ninny. What possible chance will you ever have for such an opportunity?'* But another part of her acknowledged the warning bells. Her mum always said if something seemed too good to be true, it probably was. This most definitely reeked of 'too good to be true.' But what if it wasn't? Mr. Cummings seemed one of the nicest men she'd ever met. Had he wanted to harm her, mightn't he have already done so?

She surveyed the lavish surroundings, decision made. Too good to be true, be damned. With no position at all, she would be a fool to turn down such an offer.

"Thank you. Yes, I accept." Her heart swelled with happiness. To go from sweaty, back-breaking, potentially life-threatening work in the Garment District to a party hostess in a place like this was a dream come true.

Mr. Cummings smiled and patted her shoulder. "I'm very pleased. I think you will enjoy working for me." A mischievous smile touched his mouth. "I hope the gentleman at the diner won't mind too much that you've changed your mind."

She dropped her eyes and shook her head. "I doubt he'll give it a second thought."

"Wonderful." He reached into his breast pocket and retrieved his wallet. He pulled out two twenty dollar bills and held them out. "Here is an advance."

She jerked her gaze to his. "Advance? But, I haven't yet lifted a finger. Why would you pay me an advance?"

"You need evening dresses. I'm sure you wouldn't want to wear your own nice things to work in. And you were robbed, remember? You will need some pocket money before your salary begins." He pushed the bills into her injured hand and gently closed her fingertips over the cash. "I provide an advance for all my girls. It's part of the contract."

"Contract?"

"Yes. Just a small detail to get out of the way. Come, and we'll be set." She followed him to a small desk where he opened a drawer and withdrew a few sheets of paper, then handed them to her.

She squinted at the document, cheeks burning. Her reading skills were limited at best. She could make out most of the words, but didn't understand exactly what they meant. "Um, this part here. Where I will per-perform any tasks you dee-deem appro—"

"Appropriate?" he coaxed gently.

"Yes, deem appropriate. What does that mean exactly?"

He favored her with another of those fatherly smiles. "It simply means that, as your *employer*, I determine the tasks you perform. Such as, serving drinks, chatting with partygoers. Perhaps once in a while, I will ask you to dance with a gentleman. The usual sort of thing."

Those things didn't sound all that unpleasant. Was he being forthright with her? "Those are common tasks one might expect to perform at a party?"

"Precisely." He shared another smile and handed her a fountain pen. "Once you sign the contract, I'll take you home."

She frowned down at the paper once more. "This states that I must stay for two years. If I choose to leave your employ, I'll be required to pay a fee of…" She looked up at him. "Does this say one thousand dollars?" Even with the generous salary Oscar was offering, it would take years to save that amount.

"Yes, but that's simply standard language in the agreement. It protects my investment and assures that my employees do not take the advance and then up and disappear on me."

That made sense. He had to cover his investments. Besides, why wouldn't she want to do this for two years? It sounded divine. "This is all very generous."

"Would you be able to start, say, two nights from now? I'm hosting a party, and I would love your assistance."

He seemed sincere. Nothing at all like Lord Renwald. She'd learned to recognize lechery in a man's gaze. She nodded, still not quite believing the luck that had turned her way. "I am absolutely available two nights from now. Where do I sign?"

http://aliciadean.com

Runaway

Krysta Scott

One

New York City, 1924

GRIMLY, DETECTIVE FELIX NOBLE glanced from the dead woman lying in the filthy alley to the small crowd gathered around. A slender, ivory-skinned woman with reddish blonde hair caught his attention. Her horrified expression and delicate frame elicited a strange urge to take her in his arms and offer comfort. Ridiculous. He was on the job, and he didn't even know the dame. He forced his attention back to the victim. Jaw tight, he squatted next to her. The skimpy clothing and thick make up indicated she might be a tart. The strangulation marks on her throat suggested she'd pissed off the wrong person.

It was too much to hope he'd have enough evidence to solve this one. His last two cases had gone unsolved, and the department was losing faith in him. But even worse, every time he failed, he disappointed his mentor.

"I'll find your killer," he whispered. "I swear." He hoped he could keep his promise, but knew in his heart he most likely couldn't.

LADY CHARLOTTE LEIGHTON SQUEEZED through the tightly packed tables at Club 501, swaying to Alyce Kutcher's music. The woman commanded the luxurious speakeasy, as her sexy voice drifted from the stage, augmented by the trumpet's clear notes. Charli, far from her English roots, placed drinks in front of enthusiastically clapping patrons, wide grins and flushed faces indicating how enthralled they were with the songstress. As pleasant as the sound was, Alyce could never top Meggie. Her voice wasn't near as warm. It was more strident. Imperious. Meggie—Lady Margaret as she was becoming known throughout NYC—was one of Charli's three housemates. All three had adjusted better to America than Charli. Meggie found her niche singing, Jessie landed a prime position at the *New York World*, and Eliza lucked into a posh position as party hostess, while Charli still floundered like a fish out of water. Since disembarking from the *Empress of India* six months ago, her friends had been scads more successful at accomplishing their dreams than she.

The patrons' foot stomps and flinging arms beat in a lively response to the music. Silver shoes partnered with black spats bounced through the Charleston. Flashes of brilliant blue, green, red and orange sparkled off fringed gowns.

Charli's throat tightened. Too loud. Too bright. Too crowded. She hated crowds. All that body heat, sweat and nudging. But at least staying busy kept her mind off the poor girl who'd been found murdered. Who would have done such a thing? And so close to the club…

She banished the image from her mind. Dwelling on the tragedy would help no one. Sucking in her stomach, she pushed through a narrow opening between tables, balancing a tray of drinks, careful not to spill the contents. It was one of the speakeasy rules: spill a drink, pay the tab. And she couldn't possibly afford that.

For now, she was a common drudge. A waitress. Invisible but always present. Wasn't that the story of her life? She hadn't run away from an impending forced marriage to Geoffrey Hare, only to become a waitress. However, Mrs. Greensley's Finishing school failed in offering her *practical* skills. Charli let out a dejected sigh. With no other skills, cocktail waitress seemed the best stepping stone for her ambitions.

Ah, how she missed her morning chocolate lying abed; the long constitutionals in the quiet gardens of her family homestead in England; reading for hours on end in the parlor then sneaking downstairs to assist the cook, Mrs. Erickson. She would have stayed there forever but for her meddling parents despairing over their reclusive daughter. Charli could barely bring herself to communicate with the opposite sex. She had *no* desire to marry. Instead of honoring her wishes, they'd contracted her to a stranger. *With your temperament, how will you ever make a match on your own?* The memory of her mother's harsh words stung even now though Charli was safely ensconced across the pond.

"Hey Charli." A man with ruddy cheeks and mussed brown hair smacked her on the bum. The burn radiated up her left hip, and heat flooded her face. She was self-conscious enough in the uniform—a cream-colored satin apron over a short burgundy dress with sheer voile skirt from hem to the tops of her high heels—without these bounders putting their hands on her. Unfortunately, pawing came with the position.

Gripping the tray on her shoulder, she offered a weak smile.

"Get me another gin will ya, doll?"

"Right away, sir." She couldn't remember the regular's name. That was the problem with this place. Too many faces. How could she possibly keep track of them all? She skirted between two seats, lifting her tray of precious, illegal cargo above their heads. Club 501, the most glamorous speakeasy in New York City, served only liquor imported from Europe. No cheap backwoods booze here.

Laughter bounded off every corner of the dimly lit room. The Bernie-Edison Orchestra performed, each pounding note a hammer to her head. The mob beat on the tabletops in melodic time. Even her own footsteps grabbed the annoying rhythm.

On each pass to another table, she was nudged, groped, fairly accosted. Everyone living the high life but her. She approached a table where a brassy blonde with curls plastered against her head leaned into the man at her side. He draped an arm around her and whispered into her ear. The woman tittered. Charli lowered a glass in front of him, heat flooding her cheeks. Such overt displays were unseemly. His fingers curled around the glass, but his gaze never left his date. Bah! Americans.

"Um, sir, that will be one pound—I mean dollar."

He looked up grudgingly and dug in his pocket for the cash.

She snatched it up and picked her way back to the bar. Rubbing her temples, Charli readied for the reload. Two more hours until she could bake again. She slammed the tray on the counter and blew out an aggravated breath.

"Tough night, Charli?"

She looked up to find Dollie Carter at the bar. The petite woman, dressed in a form fitting suit revealing curves Charli would never possess, soft brown hair folded neatly beneath a rounded hat, pulled her kid gloves off, fingertip by fingertip. She sat straight-backed on the barstool. Completely at ease in this atmosphere.

"Mrs. Carter," Charli choked out. Now this was one regular Charli did keep track of. The successful department store owner liked her whiskey neat. "Your usual?"

Charli stepped behind the bar and pulled a bottle from underneath and poured her customer a shot. Mrs. Carter tossed it back. Like a practiced man.

Charli glanced over at Ira. The bartender was engaged in conversation with another customer. It would be a few minutes before he filled her tray. Might as well put the time to good use and get some tips on opening her own business. Her flatmates were always telling her she had to make opportunities for herself just like Jess had secured herself a job at the *World*, even though they had thought she was a man. Charli grabbed a cloth and wiped the counter top. Without making eye contact with Mrs. Carter she said, "How is business?"

"Good." She slid her glass to Charli. Once it had been refilled, she drained it as quickly as the first one. "I'm thinking of expanding."

"Really?" Charli poured another swig, heart thudding. "Expansion?"

This time she took small, feminine sips. "Not certain. A café perhaps."

"That serves food?" The words spilled out before she could stop them. She bit her lip. Mrs. Carter would think her a ninny like everyone else. Donning her most business like expression, she studied the older woman. Mrs. Carter leveled a shrewd gaze on her. Her deep brown eyes held curiosity.

"Is there any other kind?" she said dryly.

Charli's cheeks heated, and she moved her hand swiftly over the deep cherry wood. "It sounds exciting."

"It won't be large." Mrs. Carter focused on a distant point. "I envision something in the center of the store."

This was her chance. *A bakery? A bakery would be lovely.*

"Charli." Ira's rough voice carried through the cacophony from the other side of the bar. Charli stiffened and faced his direction. He sauntered over and leaned against the counter's edge, mouth set in a disapproving grimace. "Are ya a dewdropper, Brit? Table nine is waiting."

"Indeed." She lifted the newly filled tray, and with an apologetic smile to Mrs. Carter, wove through the throng.

Ira's voice floated after her. "Don't mind her."

She glanced back over her shoulder. His wide wolf grin had grabbed Mrs. Carter's attention. Any chance to make a good impression faded in the dazzling glow of Ira's scorn.

"For a mouse she can be such a busybody. Head's always filled with zany ideas. She wanted me to serve *scones*." He barked out a laugh. "Imagine *scones* in a drinking establishment."

The weight on her shoulders dipped. She saved the load and hurried through the crowd…well, as fast as the mob would allow. Would she never be taken seriously? *The land of opportunity*. Ha. More like Land of Excess and Squander. An elbow nudged her. A red-haired man adjusted his seat closer to a brazen brunette. The woman screeched a lilt of laughter and placed a hand on his shoulder. "Careful Gustave." Her blue eyes flickered in Charli's direction. "With all the effort she's taking to serve the tables, you don't want to upset her tray, do ya pet?"

Charli nodded and rushed past. The air was thick with the nauseating odor of sweat and libations. She took a breath but couldn't seem to fill her lungs. The weight of the tray burned a line of tension down her arm causing it to shake. Just a few more feet until she could empty her tray. *An eternity*. If she could get back fast enough, she could continue her conversation with Ms. Carter. How many opportunities would she allow to pass?

Long thin fingers curled around a glass and lifted it from the tray. Charli followed the direction of the drink. Derrick Chaunce, or as the local duffs referred to him, "Slick," grinned, exposing yellowed teeth.

"You … You…" Her throat closed. The rest of her diatribe wouldn't budge.

He winked. His thin hair slicked back in the latest fashion exaggerated the gaunt cheekbones and sunken eyes tinging him with an unhealthy, dilapidated look. He gulped the whiskey. A bit of the amber liquid escaped through the gap in his teeth and down his chin. Her stomach lurched.

"Thank you, sweet cakes. Put it on my tab." He skulked off.

Charli whirled around. How did the bounder get past Tiny? Ira fumed about customers who ran up a high tab without reconciling at the end of the night. Now she would have to explain yet another charge added to Slick's mounting debt. She sighed and rolled her eyes to the heavens. The customer was always right. Even when they were wrong.

Table twenty-six overflowed with eight people crushed around the small area. The top was littered with empty glasses. She replaced empty glasses with fresh drinks. By the time she reached customer eight, the tray had no drinks left thanks to Slick's sticky fingers.

Number eight's red eyes glowered.

"Pardon, sir." Her voice squeaked. "I'll have a fresh one to you straight away." She fled. The sooner she completed his order, the sooner he would forget her incompetence. Charli searched for Ms. Carter on her way back to the bar, but the seat was empty. Gone. Another opportunity, *lost*. She blinked back tears. Would she never learn? She filled a glass with gin. Slick sidled up to the bar and reached for the glass, his lopsided grin grotesque against his sallow skin. A large hand gripped his wrist.

"What the hell do you think you're doing?" Ira glared at him. "You're cut off until you pay up."

"Awe, come on," Slick sniffed. "I'm good for it."

Ira leaned closer. "Tell that to Frank. You haven't paid your tab for three days."

Ira signaled the bouncer, Tiny, a bulky man with a balding pate and a lip curled in distaste. He nodded and made his way toward Slick. Slick's face crumpled into a pout. His eyes met Charli's, silently pleading with her. But what could she do? She shrugged and whisked the drink away to a paying customer. Even if she wanted to help the lout, Ira was the boss and there was no contradicting *him*. The farther she moved away from the clash of wills, the easier she breathed. After delivering the drink, she snuck to the hallway that led to the ladies room and leaned against the wall. Her feet throbbed. Just a short break before her next round, she promised. She glanced at her watch.

One more hour. The ache traveled up her legs. She sucked in a breath and squared her shoulders. She could walk through hell if she knew she would get out. One hour wasn't so bad, but how many more days would she have to endure before life truly began?

She had dreams. She'd stood on the deck of the *Empress of India* staring at Ellis Island, seeing her Liberty. Arms stretched wide, beckoning. Welcoming *her*. She'd seen the promise of a new beginning. It glinted off the Hudson River. But that silver chalice of freedom, once bright and shiny, was now dull and tarnished.

http://krystascottauthor.com

Other Books
by Kathy L Wheeler

The Mapmaker's Wife
(To Love A Spy Boxed Set)

The Bloomington Series
Quotable
Maybe It's You
Lies That Bind

A Tales of the Scrimshaw Doll
The Color of Betrayal (2012 The Wild Rose Press)

Books by Kae Elle Wheeler
Cinderella Series
The Wronged Princess – book i
The Unlikely Heroine – book ii
The Surprising Enchantress – book iii

The Price of Scorn – book iv

A Tales of the Scrimshaw Doll
The English Lily (2013 The Wild Rose Press)

About the Author

Kathy L Wheeler, author of both contemporary and historical romance was born in Presque Isle, Maine. She grew up in Dallas, Texas but migrated to Boulder then Longmont, Colorado where she attended high school. Her college degree from the University of Central Oklahoma is a BA in Management Information Systems and vocal music minor.

Kathy is an active member of the Oklahoma Romance Writers. Kathy also belongs to The Beau Monde and DARA chapters. She loves the NFL, holds NBA Thunder season basketball tickets and Celebrity Attractions Broadway season tickets as she also adores musical theater. Reading and writing, of course—and just to round things out and to scratch the singing itch—karaoke.

Kathy lives in Edmond, Oklahoma with her musically-talented, attorney husband, Al. They have one grown daughter and one bossy cat, Carly, who acts as if she was the *rescuer* rather than the *rescue-ee*!

Web site/blog: **http://kathylwheeler.com**
twitter: **http://twitter.com/kathylwheeler**
facebook: **http://facebook.com/kathylwheeler**
pinterest: **http://pinterest.com/kathylwheeler**
email: **kathy@klwheeler.com**

Made in the USA
San Bernardino, CA
17 February 2018